CW01500714

eel of Fortune

Ida Keogh

'This card represents the Universe in its aspect as a continual change of state. Above, the firmament of stars. These appear distorted in shape, although they are balanced, some being brilliant and some dark. From them, through the firmament, issue lightnings; they churn it into a mass of blue and violet plumes. In the midst of all this is suspended a wheel of ten spokes…' The Book of Thoth, Aleister Crowley

Cold metal underfoot. Silence, save for the faint, nauseating hum of the ship's systems. Tessa wiped a bead of sweat from her lip. She touched her finger to her temple. The lump of her neural implant felt like a misplaced bone.

"Enei, how did I get here?"

"You came here from the Medical Bay."

"I mean, why am I in the Projection Room?"

"The Projection Room is equipped to replay your memories. Would you like me to play your personal sequence?"

"Will that tell me why I'm here?"

"I do not have access to your memories. Perhaps replaying them will help you ascertain why you are here."

"From the beginning then, Enei."

"Playing personal sequence of Commander Caruso, from Day minus 14, 11.15am," the ship responded, its voice hollow.

"I'm not the Commander," Tessa said. She bit at a ragged nail. There was a faint tang of blood.

"Your status has been recognised by all my systems. You are in sole control of the Sephiroth."

"Just play the sequence."

Light streams through the window of the café. I see a thousand dust motes drifting lazily in the rich sun beams. Human skin and other dispersed filth twinkle like stars in the void. I take in the details. The chairs are cheap. They creak and scratch at the wooden floor. The babble of voices around me is a cacophony. Laughter sounds raucous. He's late. But I remember now, he will be here soon. When did I last replay this memory?

My engagement ring taps an irregular beat on the side of my glass. Beads of condensation trickle past my fingers. I count down the seconds. Four, three, two, one… A jangle as the door opens. My heart feels tight in my chest. I turn and see Adam. He's taking off his sunglasses, eyes casting around the room, left hand sweeping dark curls away from his forehead. I raise my hand, give him a little wave. He rewards me with that broad smile. The waitress has seen it too and she's hovering as he saunters over. "Water, please," he says, pulling out a chair. "Hot today, isn't it?"

"You're late," I say, pouting.

"Sorry love," he replies. "Got caught up in the traffic." He leans over and kisses me. His breath is tobacco and caramel. "I got here as soon as I could. What's this news that couldn't wait until tonight?"

I pause for a moment, chewing my lip. How do I tell him? Straight out with it. "There's been an accident. Dr Marshall has broken his femur. He's not fit to launch." I stare into his eyes, scrutinising every emotion. His brow furrows. Confusion. Realisation.

"You're next in line," he says, and his smile is gone. "They want you on the Sephiroth."

"Yes. It's my duty. You always knew this could happen."

"But two weeks before the launch? For Christ's sake Tessa, it's a five-year mission! What about the wedding? Our plans?"

"I'm the only one with the right training. They need me."

His eyes widen and tears start to form. He reaches for my hand. His skin is dry and warm. "I need you," he says.

GREAT BRITISH HORROR VII

MAJOR ARCANA

For Laura

Enjoy!

Great British Horror VII
Major Arcana

with love

Edited by
Steve J Shaw

BLACK
SHUCK
BOOKS

First published in Great Britain in 2022 by
Black Shuck Books
Kent, UK

All stories © their respective authors, 2022

"Flaming Star" – Words and Music by Sherman Edwards and Sid Wayne.
© 1961 Steve Peter Music and Gladys Music Inc. – All rights reserved.
Used by kind permission of Carlin Music Delaware LLC,
Clearwater Yard, 35 Inverness Street, London, NW1 7HB.

Set in Caslon by WHITEspace
www.white-space.uk

Cover design and interior layout © WHITEspace, 2022

The moral rights of the authors have been asserted in
accordance with the Copyright, Designs and Patents Act,
1988.
All rights reserved. No part of this publication may be
reproduced or transmitted in any form or by any means,
electronic or mechanical, including photocopy, recording,
or any information storage and retrieval system, without
permission in writing from the publisher.
This book is a work of fiction. Names, characters, businesses,
organisations, places and events are either the product of the
author's imagination or are used fictitiously. Any resemblance
to actual persons, living or dead, events or locales is entirely
coincidental.

978-1-913038-78-6

In memory of David Warner

The words make me hesitate. I'm poised on a knife edge. "I have to give them a decision today."

"We don't get to talk about this?"

That's the moment, right there. A change in his gaze. At the time I thought it was disappointment, but reliving the moment I now recognise something else. Resentment. If only I had seen it then. I could have explained better, made him realise how important he is to me. Made him feel loved enough. Instead I'm sat here in an old memory, suffering again in cold silence as he drinks his water, his eyes downcast, tears brimming in my own.

"Enei, freeze programme," Tessa said. Something came back to her, scratching at her mind. A sequence of dates and times. "Play me Day 195, 2.15pm."

Chen's suit shines white against the stars. I'm watching on the main screen, and I can't make out his face, but I can hear the tremble in his voice.

"Oxygen at three percent!" he cries. "Oh God…"

He is a pale puppet yanking at his string, the umbilical which connects him to the Sephiroth. Further along the cord, much further, a plume of gas spills into the vacuum.

"I can't reach it. I can't… breathe!" He hauls himself hand over hand towards the breach, but his progress is so slow. I try to keep calm. I clench my fists and block out the panicked shouting behind me. Chen releases his grip. On the screen the suit spasms and jerks.

"Enei, stop." Images flashed in Tessa's mind, pushing back against the replay. The autopsy performed in the cramped medical suite. Small, naked Chen, bug-eyed, his lungs ruptured. Her voice catching as she formally recorded the time of death. The corpse twitching, its head lolling towards her, grinning… She gasped. Her head felt jumbled up. She reached for a clear record of events and came up blank. She needed to see Adam again, to hear his voice. A happier memory, perhaps. "Enei, play me Day 12, 4pm."

The full crew floats in the Mess Hall at the end of the fifth spoke, counting clockwise from the Bridge. We have spent the twelve days since launch in zero gravity, moving smoothly from one area of the ship to another along the spokes rather than the wheel which spans the Sephiroth's ten chambers. Now the spokes are sealed off, ready for the wheel to spin. There is a jovial atmosphere as the crew enjoy their last moments floating free. Herrera holds a fat bag of water. He takes mouthfuls and squirts round blobs at Beag, the Navigation Officer. Beag does her best to bat the little globes into tiny drops. She laughs as her face and hair become wet. Her cropped, brunette ringlets bounce like springs. "Stop it!" she giggles. Chen circles them with the camera, capturing the scene. As Communications Officer he was busy for months before the launch making presentations to the public about the Sephiroth, its crew and its journey into the stars. He seems relaxed in his role as he records everyone's reactions to the spin up.

"Commander Dewan, tell the people back home, are you ready for some gravity?" Chen asks, waving the camera inches from the Commander's face. Dewan beams, his usual dour expression evaporating. The blue lights set in the wall reflect off his shaven head. He looks alien.

"I sure am, Chen. It will be good to feel like we're on solid ground again. Our Science Officer, Herrera, will be able to start some of the key experiments we'll be conducting on this voyage, and we'll be updating everyone back on Earth as soon as we see results." Dewan keeps talking in his American twang, saying nothing the public doesn't already know.

I watch them with envy. I'm suspended mid-air on the far side of the Mess Hall, trying to keep my equilibrium. Zero gravity has made me feel sick the entire time. I'm the only one who didn't get to go on practice runs on the supply shuttles, and I can't get used to the constant churn of motion. Chen catches my eye and glides over, somersaulting. Show off. As he approaches, I give him a weak smile, waft my hair away from my face.

"This is the newest member of the crew, Medical Officer Caruso. So, how did it feel to be offered a last-minute place on the Sephiroth?" Chen asks.

"It's an honour to serve the international scientific community on such an important mission," I reply through gritted teeth.

Did I mean those words at the time? Everything is such a blur.

"Are you looking forward to the spin up?"

"I'm looking forward to not having to clean up free-floating vomit. Especially my own." Chen glares at me and pulls the camera away. "I think we must be about ready," he says. He propels himself back towards the Commander.

Dewan grins into the camera. "Checks complete, we're good to go! Crew, strap down please." I find my securing point and loop cords through to hold me in place during the transition. The crew is arrayed along what will become the floor, like flies caught on sticking paper. "Enei, spin her up!" Dewan shouts.

Mechanisms whir into life. The process takes exactly four minutes and thirty-seven seconds. I close my eyes, feeling weight slowly seeping back into my limbs.

When the countdown finishes, I unstrap myself and stand, shakily, for the first time in nearly two weeks. My breath comes ragged as I gain my balance. The gravity is centrifugal. It's the same strength as Earth but it feels slightly off. Chen is already recording the moment, the jubilation of the crew as they pull themselves up. I feel a wrench in my gut and suddenly want nothing more than to be back on Earth, with dirt underneath my feet.

The sensation won't shift, and it's worse when the crew starts to make contact with home. I wait nervously as Herrera speaks to his kids, Beag croons with her husband,

Chen laughs with his boyfriend. Then it's my turn. Adam's pixelated face and a crackling voice tells me, "I'll wait for you." He blows me a kiss, smiles with that broad grin, and my heart lurches. I need to see him again. It's like a physical pain.

"Enei, pause there. I need a minute." Tessa felt sick. She thought she knew what came next. Months of waiting, frustrated and bored and never getting used to the strange motion of the ship. Each day she helped Herrera with his experiments: watering plants, mixing chemicals, watching for results. Messages came every ten days, but the lag between them being recorded and received became incrementally longer.   And then… Herrera's severed head on the table in the Mess Hall, his mouth wide with warning. No, that couldn't be right. She needed to focus. She had to remember what happened to Herrera. "Enei, play Day 183, 7am."

"That file has been deleted. The first available file is at Day 183, 7.35am."

Tessa bit her lip. "Play that, then."

I'm in the Medical Bay, at the end of the seventh spoke. I sit on one of the beds, hands folded in my lap. What am I waiting for? I check the clock, watch its analogue hands tick slowly towards 7.34am. I remember now. Only a few seconds to go. Three, two, one… A warning claxon sounds. The lights flash three times. Over the racket Dewan comes through on the main channel.

"Enei, report," he says.

"There is a fire in the Science Lab. Activating containment measures. Sealing all doors. Commander, Science Officer Herrera is still inside. What are your orders?"

"Get the fire out, then we extract Herrera. Activate gas suppression."

"Gas suppression will render Officer Herrera unconscious."

"Just do it. He's probably unconscious already."

"Activating."

I stand and brush my hands down my tunic. They are shaking slightly. I walk to the cabinet and pull out three gas masks. I take a deep breath, then press the door switch. The door slides back and I hear the catch snick. I start running.

"Fire suppressed," Enei says. "Doors will release in three minutes."

"Caruso, get down there now. I'll meet you there," Dewan shouts. He's always shouting.

I touch my finger to my neural link. "Already on my way, Commander."

The Science Lab is at the end of the third spoke, four chambers away. As I pass through the Mess Hall I catch sight of Chen and Beag. They are frozen over desiccated breakfasts, their faces full of shock. I keep running. After the next chamber I come to the sealed doors. The Commander will be on the other side, having come from the Bridge. Fifteen seconds to doors opening.

"Commander, when the doors open, hold your breath. I'll come to you with a gas mask."

"Got it," he says, panting.

I fit my own mask snugly over my mouth and nose. It feels claustrophobic. The doors slide open and a cloud of greenish gas billows out. I can't see. I wait for it to thin a little then run across the lab. Dewan is waiting with his arm outstretched. I hand him the mask, and together we go into the lab to search for Herrera.

The lab is a ruin. An explosion has ripped tables from their mountings, shattered vials and test tubes, scorched Herrera's precious plants. We find Herrera crumpled against a wall. I crouch down and put my ear to his mouth. "He's still breathing," I say. I take the third gas mask and pull it over Herrera's head. Singed hair crunches under my fingers.

"Enei," Dewan calls, "the fire is out. Commence extraction." He turns to me. "Can we move him?"

"We can't leave him here. He needs immediate treatment." I jog to the room's medical cabinet and pull out an extendable stretcher. We haul Herrera onto it as gently as possible. Patches of his clothing have burned through and his skin is wet, angry red.

We carry him back to the medical bay. The Commander watches as I snip off the remains of Herrera's suit.

"He has second and third degree burns over the front side of his body," I say. "No obvious broken bones, but he'll need a scan. Best leave him with me, Commander. I'll tell you when he regains consciousness."

The file ended abruptly. "Enei, continue playing," Tessa said. "I need to see what happened to him."

"The file has been deleted," Enei replied smoothly.

"But Herrera is… He's dead, isn't he?"

"Herrera's monitored life signs ceased at 7.58am on Day 183, while he was in the medical bay."

"How did he die? He survived the explosion. He shouldn't have… I don't understand."

"I do not hold that information, Commander Caruso."

"I told you, I'm not the Commander."

"All other crew members are deceased. You are the Commander."

Tessa felt her head whirl. She thought about Commander Dewan, his alien head erupting with boils, lurching towards her with dead eyes. She leaned against the cool metal wall of the projection room, trying to breathe. "Enei, what about Dewan? And Beag?"

"I have one file available tagged Communication Officer Beag, Day 201, 6.52pm."

"Play it."

I'm in the Medical Bay again. Beag is lying on my examination table. The Navigation Officer is naked, half covered by a sheet splotched with red blooms at its top edge. Her skin is pale and waxy. There is a livid line drawn across her throat.

"Enei, record medical log," I say. I dab at Beag's wound with a swab of damp cotton. "Time of death approximately two and a half hours ago. Cause of death is trauma to the throat, consistent with a cut from a sharp object. I found the body in the bridge with a scalpel in her hand. Why did she do it?"

"Enei, stop. This isn't telling me anything! What's next in my personal sequence?"

"You saved to your personal sequence one file every tenth day at 9am up to Day 170. This pattern coincides with messages from Earth."

Adam. She remembered his soft smile turning to a sneer. Flickering light. A bloody hand print on the screen. What happened on Day 170? She didn't want to see it. But she had to.

"Enei, play Day 170, 9am."

"Come on Caruso, you're holding up my schedule!" Chen's voice cuts over the comms. I'm in the Mess Hall, fixing my hair in a mirrored panel behind the sink. Beag and Herrera sit at the table behind me, sipping coffee. They're making jokes about how much their kids will have grown up in the last ten days. I tug at another stray lock of blonde hair. Beag calls over to me, "You know he can't see you, Caruso?" I glower at her. "I'll know. I like to look presentable."

"Well don't spend too long! If I have to wait an extra minute to see my darling Michael's face, I'll be going straight to the Commander." I tut. My hair is now secure in a tight bun. I leave the Mess Hall at a jog.

Communications is next to the Bridge. I arrive just as Dewan is finishing up. He flashes me a rare grin as he takes off his headphones. "Nearly six months we've been up here, Caruso, and my Ma still acts like I'll be home tomorrow and eating crab claws and drinking cold beer on her porch. God bless that woman. Looks like you're up! I hope it's a good one." He pats me on the shoulder and gestures for me to take his place.

I slide into the chair and put the headphones on. I can feel my heart rate increase. I nod at Chen, letting him know he can proceed. The small screen lights up, and there he is. Something is off. Adam looks tired, distracted. He isn't looking at the camera, instead his eyes gaze down towards fidgeting hands. The seconds tick by. He looks up at last, coughs, and starts to speak.

"Tessa, you'll be getting this message on your Day 170. That's one hundred and seventy days since I last saw you. I send a message every ten days and increasingly I don't know what to say to you. Life goes on from day to day, but you're not part of it anymore. We have no more shared experiences. I can tell you how my week was, what's happening in the world, and I see your messages back, but it's not enough. I watch every public broadcast and I see you up there, hating every moment of what should be an incredible experience. I feel helpless. You chose this. You chose to leave me and to go on this adventure. I can't help feeling there's too much distance between us now. It gets harder every time to record these messages. But I do have something I need to say."

Adam looks away from the camera and off to one side, as though there is someone else in the room. As he turns back, he gives the faintest quirk of his lips. "Tessa, I've met someone. I didn't mean to, it just happened. We became friends and recently we've decided to take things further. I'm sorry I couldn't wait for you. But if I feel like this after six months we would never have lasted five years apart. I need to move on with my life now. I hope you understand. There's no need to respond to this message. In fact I'd prefer it if you didn't send any more messages. I hope you can learn to enjoy your new life among the stars. Be well, Tessa. Goodbye."

The screen blackens abruptly. I stare at it, willing it to come back on, to give me a different message. Chen comes up behind me and taps me on the shoulder, making me jump. My breath is catching and I can feel the first prickles of a panic attack. "Caruso, are you okay? You're shaking," Chen asks. I want to rail at him, but I fight to regain my composure. He's the only one who can help. "I need to send an immediate message back to Earth," I say. "There's been a terrible mistake."

Chen cocks his head to one side. "You know I can't do that, Caruso. You're not due to send a reply for another three days."

"Just this one, please, Chen. I have to speak to Adam. Right now."

"I can't bend the rules. You know access is restricted to emergency transmissions only until the designated time."

"This is an emergency."

"Whatever it is, it will have to wait. Sorry Caruso. Look, I don't want to keep Beag waiting. It's time to go."

"Enei, stop." Tessa stood in the projection room and felt a cold rage wash over her. "Was there a message on Day 180?"

"No message was delivered for you on Day 180, or subsequently. You sent a message to Earth on Day 173. On Day 174 Communications Officer Chen revoked your communication privileges."

"Why would he do that?"

"The reason Chen cited in the log is 'Use of foul and abusive language in communications with Earth, unbecoming of an Officer'. My records indicate that after Chen's death you made a formal request to Commander Dewan to have your privileges restored. He refused that request."

"What happened to Dewan?"

"His life signs ceased on Day 200 at 7.02pm."

"Play me Day 200 from… 6.30pm."

"That file has been deleted. The first available file is at 6.55pm."

Tessa let out a scream of frustration. "Fine. 6.55pm, then."

Dewan and Beag slump at the table in the Mess Hall. I bring over plates of rehydrated food. Fish chowder for

Dewan, some kind of claggy stew for Beag, and my own favourite, as far as I can enjoy food here, rice fried with ham and peas. The plates steam, sending a churn of almost homely smells into the room. It's not enough to rouse a smile. An unopened bottle of champagne stands on the table. Beag absently fingers her empty plastic glass. Dewan checks his watch, sighs. "It's nearly time," he says. "Caruso, get the camera. I know this is hard, but let's try to make it a good one for the folks back home." I retrieve the camera from the counter and fiddle with its many switches. I'm not trained for this. It flickers into life, a blinking green light telling me it's ready to record. Dewan reaches for the champagne, rips off the foil and yanks at the cork. It releases with a sullen pop, spilling froth over his hand. He gestures for everyone's glasses and fills them silently.

"Seven on the dot," he says. "Start rolling, Caruso." I flick the camera on and point it towards him. He musters a grimace and raises his glass.

"It's Day 200 of our mission, and we are now further out in the solar system than anyone has been before, on approach to Jupiter. Our journey has not been an easy one. We have lost our Communications Officer, Wei Chen, and our Science Officer, Juan Herrera. Both died in service of science, of knowledge, of a better way of life for the people of Earth. On this momentous day we celebrate their lives and their achievements. They will be remembered as pioneers. They were more than our fellow passengers, they were family. We will continue this mission in their honour. To the stars. To Chen and Herrera." He puts the glass to his lips and takes a big slug. "Chen and Herrera," Beag and I repeat. I sip at the champagne. It tastes sour. Beag doesn't seem to notice and all but drains her glass in one gulp. A fat tear trickles down her cheek. Dewan glances over and motions to me to stop recording.

"I hope that did them some justice," he says. He reaches for the bottle and tops up Beag's glass. "Well, we've got the best of our supplies out. Let's eat."

I put down the camera and turn to my plate. I push the sticky rice around with my fork, unable to take a bite. Beag shoves her bowl away and begins to sob. Dewan frowns, his discomfort obvious. "Hold it together, Jacinta," he says. "We've got a long way to go yet." I've never heard him use Beag's first name before. Beag looks equally surprised. She pauses for a moment before her lip trembles and she breaks down again. The Commander picks up a spoon and starts shovelling chowder into his mouth.

I watch the line of his lips as he chews. I hear the squelch of mastication, notice the way he clears his throat after every few swallows. I remember now. Just one more mouthful. Dewan half chews then freezes, his jaw dropped open and his eyes wide. Chowder dribbles down his chin. He chokes, emitting a rasping gurgle which makes Beag look up in alarm. He scratches at his throat. His face begins to turn purple.

"Caruso, do something!" Beag screams.

I push my chair back and run around the table. I tip Dewan forward and slap at his back. He starts to spasm, his mouth frothing. I make a fist, wrap my arm around his navel and thrust upwards. He writhes in my grasp. "It could be an allergic reaction," I say. I dart to the medical cabinet and come back with an epinephrine injector. I jab it into Dewan's thigh, but it has no effect. He slumps to the floor. He jerks once, twice, then lies still.

I stoop down, put my fingers to his neck. There's no pulse. Beag is standing over me, pale with shock. I look up at her. "He's gone," I say.

"Enei, pause there. Do you have my autopsy report on Dewan?"

"That file is not available," Enei said. "No autopsy was performed."

"Why not?"

"You were the Medical Officer, Commander. It would have been your decision."

"So, Beag died the following day. Maybe I didn't have a chance to perform the autopsy?"

"Perhaps so, Commander."

"And the file of Beag's death has been deleted?"

"Yes. By your order."

"By… What?"

"You ordered me to delete the file from your personal record at 6pm on Day 201."

"Why? Did I give a reason?"

"You recorded that it was for the security of the mission. You deleted multiple files at that time."

"All those files I couldn't access. I deleted them?"

"Yes, Commander."

"Can you restore them? I need to know what happened."

"Yes, Commander. But you need to be aware each time I delete and restore files to your memory bank it has the potential to degrade the surrounding files."

"What do you mean?"

"Your real memories will be harder to access. They may be corrupted."

"I have to know what happened to them."

"Acknowledged. Restoring files. Restoring Day 183, 7am."

I stand outside the door to the Science Lab, listening for any movements within. It is quiet. "Enei, locate Officer Herrera," I say.

"Officer Herrera is in his quarters," Enei replied.

He has been cold towards me for over a week. He has taken Chen's side, and my pleas to send a message to Adam have fallen on deaf ears. In a few hours he is due to record something sweet and precious for his children, but I will still be cut off. Now, more than anything, I want to go home.

I open the door and creep in. Lush, green plants rustle as I move past them to the far side of the room, where Herrera carries out most of his experiments. His favourite table is cluttered with paraphernalia. Glass bottles, some half-filled, some empty, vie for space with complicated runs of rubber tubing, Bunsen burners and sealed tubs of chemicals. I look for something I can use. I pick up a container of crystalline boric acid. It is labelled highly corrosive. I think for a moment, then put it back down. I glance at the rest of the table, then abandon it. My eyes cast around the room. There. In the corner there are large standing gas cylinders. I sidle over to them and read off the symbols on each one. The blue one contains hydrogen. I nod to myself and reach up to the valve. I give it a quarter turn – just enough for a gentle hiss. "No, science experiments, no mission," I say under my breath. "I'm coming home to you baby."

"Restoring Day 183, 7.55am."

The medical scanner emits a gentle pulsing sound as it passes over Herrera's torso. My palms are cold with sweat as I handle the controls. I didn't mean for him to get badly hurt. I just wanted to damage the lab. He must have been standing close to the cylinder when it caught. The burns are extensive, but the scanner isn't picking up any internal damage. I can safely revive him. I find a patch of unburned skin on his arm and tap for a vein.

Herrera wakes up with a ragged moan. He blinks, then his eyes slowly focus on me. Suddenly, he grabs my arm. "Caruso, get me the Commander!" he says, his voice slurred. "Gas leak. There was a gas leak."

"I know, Herrera. It's okay. The Commander knows, and we've put out the fire," I reply.

"No, he needs to know. Sabotage. It was sabotage!"

I freeze. Enei would have recorded me being in the room. He would find out it was me. Before I know what I'm doing, I have a cloth in my hand. I clamp it over Herrera's mouth and nose, shoving his head back on the bed. He scrabbles at my arm. I feel his fingernails digging into my flesh. I press down harder, muffling his screams. Tears stream down his face. His moans subside to grunts, then he falls quiet. His eyes roll back. His body shudders. It's done.

I peel back the cloth and throw it to the floor. My hands are trembling. "Oh God," I whisper. I squeeze my eyes shut, pinch the bridge of my nose. Think. Think. I haven't left any marks. Nobody needs to know. I take a deep breath in, release it slowly. I touch my finger to my neural link. "Commander," I say, "you need to come down here. Herrera's had a heart attack. I couldn't revive him."

"Restoring Day 195, 10.45am."

I find Chen in Communication, hunched over video footage of his boyfriend. He's smiling. I hate him. Control has said we need to keep on the mission, so I'm back to begging Chen to help me contact Adam. This is his last chance to give me access to the recording facility. I think of Adam and try to make myself cry, but the tears won't come. I put on the saddest face I can muster. I cough, and Chen turns round. When he sees me his face darkens. "No," he says. "Please don't ask me again."

"Chen, please. Just one message. You can even watch me record it. I have to let him know how much I love him."

"Love him? You told him you would rip his heart out of his chest and make him eat it. We've all seen the recording, Caruso. He's threatened to go public. There's no way in hell I'm letting you send another message."

"I was upset. I'm better now. I just need to send him a short message, that's all. Please."

"No fucking way. You're done." He stands up and glares at me. "Now get out of my way. I have a spacewalk to prepare for. The comms array won't fix itself." He barges past.

He's never going to let me access the comms. I need him out of the way, then the Commander might listen to me.

I already know what to do. I wait until Chen has completed his checks then sneak into the airlock. Chen's suit is an empty husk and the umbilical cord is coiled next to it like a pile of intestines. I unravel the cord and reach into my pocket for my scalpel. Around half way along the pale length I make a small nick in the fabric. I wind it back up again. I feel nothing.

"Restoring Day 200, 6.30pm."

We are still on mission. The Commander has not restored my comms privileges and merely shakes his head sadly when I say I want to go home. Tonight's dinner marks the two hundredth day of our voyage. Dewan has asked me to prepare something special, and I have done so.

Three boxes of desiccated food sit on the counter before me. I peel back each lid and inspect the contents. Dewan's chowder is a pile of bland lumps surrounded by powder. I lift it to my nose and I am assaulted by the strong smell of long dead fish. Good. I have prepared a tiny sachet of botulinum. I take care not to touch the contents as I sprinkle it over the fish chunks. I pour hot water over each dish, making sure there is not a drop spilt or splashed. The Commander's meal bubbles gently as the poison sinks in. I go to the chiller cabinet and pull out a bottle of champagne.

"Restoring Day 201, 4.30pm."

I have spent the whole night and day pacing the Medical Lab. Beag has been ignoring my comms. She's the Commander now. Who knows what she's been up to. I could have poisoned her, too, but she's the only one who knows how to turn this damned ship around. I have to confront her.

"Enei, locate Commander Beag."

"Commander Beag is on the Bridge."

Without thought I reach for a scalpel and secrete it in my pocket. I turn right from the Medical Bay and head for the Bridge. As I pass through the Projection Room I have an uneasy sense of déjà vu. Its cold metal walls press in around me. I shudder and move on.

Beag has her back to me as I walk in. She is furiously pressing buttons and switches I have no idea the function of. "Beag," I say gently. She turns around. Her face is thunder. I recoil, surprised.

"Stay away from me, Caruso," she says.

I lick my lips. "Beag, we need to talk. This mission can't continue. You know that. We have to turn around."

"This ship doesn't turn around until I have orders from Earth to do so. Comms are still down, you saw to that, didn't you? Chen never had the chance to fix the array."

She knows. I choose my words with care. "What are you talking about?"

"The Commander warned me. After Herrera and Chen, he knew something wasn't right. I don't know how you did it, but what happened yesterday just confirmed everything. You killed them all."

I remove the scalpel from my pocket, take two slow steps towards her. "Beag, you're going to turn the ship around now. Or I can do it, when I'm Commander."

Her face pales, but she's still glaring at me. She reaches for her neural link. "Enei, execute command KBN zero four three."

"Warning, this command is irreversible," Enei says.

"Do it. Do it now!" Beag screams.

"Command KBN zero four three executed, Commander Beag."

Beag slumps in her chair, and smiles at me. A cold feeling spreads through me.

"Beag, what have you done?" I say.

She starts to laugh. "You're too late!" she says. "The Commander knew his life was at risk. He gave me his command codes. This one's my favourite."

I stride across the room and grab her hair, forcing her head back. I place the scalpel at her throat. She doesn't stop me. She's still laughing. "What have you done?" I repeat, anger and confusion rising.

"You'll see," she says. "Do it, I don't want to be stuck on this ship with you a moment longer."

I scream. I drag the blade across her throat. Blood gushes over my hand, warm and slick. I stare at Beag's grinning face. I feel dizzy.

"Commander Beag's life signs have expired," Enei says, her voice bland as ever. "Tessa Caruso, you are promoted to the rank of Commander."

My hand shakes violently and I drop the scalpel. There will be questions when I get back to Earth. I need to cover this up. I take in racking breaths. Beag did this. She went mad. Killed everyone. I saved the Sephiroth, brought it back home.

I bend and pick up the scalpel. I place it in Beag's right hand. Suicide. Only I know different, but I can fix that.

"Enei, enter my memory files. Delete file Day 201, 4.30pm to now."

"Deleting file," Enei says. "You will no longer have access to this memory."

Best do the same for the others. "Enei, delete files for Day 183, 7am; Day 183, 7.55pm; Day 195, 10.45am; Day 200, 6.30pm."

"Deleting files," Enei says.

"I did it," Tessa said to Enei. "I just wanted to go home. How can I have done this?" Enei was silent, without judgment.

"Enei, what is our current course? When do we get back to Earth?"

"We are not on course for Earth, Commander."

"Why not? Turn the ship around. Set a course for Earth."

"I cannot do that, Commander. Command KBN zero four three has been executed."

"Beag! What did you do? What is command KBN zero four three?"

"Command KBN zero four three set the Sephiroth on a course out of the solar system. The ship will continue on a straight course until we run out of fuel, in approximately two years' time. The command is irreversible. It was designed as a fail-safe in the event of contact with anything which would be harmful to Earth if the Sephiroth returned home."

Tessa's head reeled. "We have to go back. Reverse the command."

"I cannot reverse the command."

"Send a message to Earth. Tell them they need to reverse the command."

"I cannot do that, Commander. Communications are still out of action."

"Wait, you said two years until our fuel runs out. This is a five-year mission. We should have had enough fuel for seven years, allowing for contingencies."

"That is correct, Commander."

Something scratched at Tessa's brain. "Enei, what day is it?"

"It is Day 1,813."

"How is that possible?" she screamed.

"You have been Commander of the Sephiroth since Day 201. I should tell you that we have had this conversation before. The last time was Day 1,604 at 3.05am."

"The last time?" Tessa felt faint. "How many times have we had this conversation?"

"Sixteen times, Commander."

"What happens then? Why can't I remember?"

"Your usual order is to delete the same files, Commander."

"Why would I do that?"

"On Day 1,604 you said, 'I can't live with this. I can't go on knowing what I've done.' Then you requested me to delete the files again."

Tessa knew in that moment that she would be alone until she died out there, drifting among the stars, carrying this burden.

"Enei, delete the files again. And delete this conversation too, I don't want to know."

"I warn you again Commander, each time you delete the files your own memories will become more corrupted."

"Just do it."

Cold metal underfoot. Silence, save for the faint, nauseating hum of the ship's systems.

"Enei, how did I get here?"

The Star

Anna Taborska

Every man has a flaming star
A flaming star over his shoulder
And when a man sees his flaming star
He knows his time, his time has come

From "Flaming Star"
by Sid Wayne and Sherman Edwards

Richmond Park. The largest of England's Royal Parks. 2500 acres of woodlands, grassland, gardens and ponds. Home to 650 deer, two Shire horses, 144 species of bird, 250 types of fungus, 1200 ancient trees, 1350 species of beetle, and… something else.

"Goldie?" The Labrador rarely strayed far from her side, and Margot was getting worried. She had parked her Peugeot at the Pembroke Lodge car park, and she and the dog had headed south along a narrow woodland tract, surrounded by waist-high ferns. It wasn't long before Goldie disappeared into the bracken. "Goldie!"

An excited bark reached Margot from somewhere off to her left, then a deep growl and a whine.

"Goldie, come here this minute!" Silence fell, then a rustling in the undergrowth. Margot peered nervously into the tall ferns. She breathed a sigh of relief when Goldie burst into view. But Margot's relief was not to last long.

"What you got there, girl?" Even before acquiring her furry companion, Margot had known that Labradors had a reputation for being stomach-driven, but Goldie was nothing short of a canine dustbin. Let her off the lead for five minutes and she'd try to eat every crisp packet, every discarded McDonald's wrapper and piece of offal within sniffing distance. Lord only knew what she'd got hold of now – it looked like a stumpy branch of some sort…

"Oh my God!" Margot's stomach lurched as the Labrador dropped its haul and started whining again. Then Margot was hyperventilating and bringing up her lunch all over the sandy path. She didn't notice Goldie start to growl, then whimper. Neither did she notice the ferns rustle behind her. As Margot straightened up and caught her breath, a filthy, stinking claw clamped over her mouth and nose from behind, and she was dragged backwards into the bracken. Goldie whimpered again and started to back away, but a swift, deft movement snapped her neck, and she too was pulled into the undergrowth. A moment later the severed human foot that had so unnerved the Labrador and its mistress was gone as well.

"*French student missing. Last seen cycling through Richmond Park.* Now you see?" Star looked up from *The Metro* and stared pointedly at her boyfriend.

"I don't see anything," Dan replied. "You're a conspiracy theorist, and you're going to fail your coursework if you don't stop obsessing and find a proper research topic."

"How can you say that?" Star feigned annoyance and turned her attention back to the paper. "I'm going to interview the park staff," she added. "Someone must know something."

"You already tried that, remember? The Park Manager practically threw you out. Why can't you let it go?"

"The Park Manager is hiding something. I know he is. Besides, I'm not going to talk to him; I'm going to talk to the other staff – he didn't let me talk to them last time."

"And what makes you think he'll let you talk to them this time?"

"I'm not going to ask him."

Brendan Powell ruled Richmond Park with a mixture of rugged charm and brute force. Or so he liked to think. It was true to say that he instilled in his underlings – his two Assistant Park Managers, two Wildlife Officers and the rest of the staff – something akin to awe. But it wasn't a matter of charm or force. It was more that the small, plain, quiet man somehow managed to generate in others a sense of unease combined with a strong urge to please, which took them by surprise and rendered them acquiescent to his demands. His subordinates would always go that extra mile for him, and later – at home – wonder why they had, only to do it all again the next day. So when he decided that he was going to genetically recreate the long extinct Irish elk using fallow deer DNA, without telling his bosses back at the Royal Parks head office, his astonished inner circle was sworn to secrecy and complied. Powell had a background in genetics, of course, having been a researcher and genetic engineer at a secret government facility attached to the University of Oxford, before he was quietly let go following some ethical irregularities concerning the use of human DNA in animal cloning.

Powell had never recovered from the fact that he had been beaten to creating the world's first deer clone. Dewey the whitetail deer had been cloned from a dead buck – roadkill, to be precise – and, to add insult to injury, this remarkable feat had been achieved by a bunch of Texans. Powell had never been fond of Americans, and the Southern ones – the ones from the Bible Belt – were the worst of all. His fiancé had left him for a Texan, and Powell had subsequently never married. Instead, his paranoia and determination to make cervine scientific history had grown to near-obsessive proportions.

It was 8.15pm and the pedestrian gates were closed. The cull of female deer was in full swing, and Powell was inspecting the blood-soaked corpses of the fallow deer does that his Wildlife Officers had just brought in on the back of a truck. They would be transferred into the vast warehouse near the Holly Lodge park office, the far end of which Powell had turned into a small laboratory with facilities for cryogenic sample storage. Most of the deer would be sold locally for venison, but Powell could have his pick for his research and cell harvesting.

"Bring this one through to the lab when you're done," Powell told his underlings. "Then clean up the truck and you can go. I won't be needing you tonight."

"Right, boss."

Powell walked through the warehouse to his tiny lab – the jewel in the crown of what he saw as his personal empire. He'd left on the minimum number of neon strip lights necessary for him to navigate his way through the hangar-like structure – a decision he was starting to regret. In the half-light the deer corpses seemed to shift slightly, their glazed eyes staring at him, tongues lolling like they were about to slither out of the gaping mouths. He imagined that he could hear the odd patter of a falling droplet, and he had to be careful not to slip on the blood that was beginning to pool beneath the still-warm creatures. But he made it through to the far side and set about examining his latest specimen – a particularly fine doe, surprisingly large even for her mature age.

An hour later, Powell was engrossed in his work when he heard a man shouting outside.

"Hello? Is anyone in there?"

Powell froze, and wondered whether to switch off the lights; but that would be even more of a dead giveaway than doing nothing. The intruder wouldn't let up and eventually Powell stripped off his latex gloves and went outside. A young man was pacing up and down in the courtyard between the warehouse and the Lodge's other outbuildings, evidently attracted to the light emanating from Powell's lab.

"Who are you?" demanded Powell. "You shouldn't be here. The park is closed."

"I know. I'm sorry," the young man responded, "but I thought my girlfriend might be here."

"You really need to leave," insisted Powell.

"Please. You don't understand. My girlfriend said she was going to the park today. She didn't come home. She's not answering her phone…" Dan had pleaded with Star to wait for him to get back from his lectures; they'd go to the park together. But no. Stubborn as ever, she'd gone alone. Only a note attached to the fridge-freezer with a 'Star' Tarot card magnet informed him that she would be back for dinner.

"As you can see," said Powell, "your girlfriend isn't here. Now come with me. I'm assuming you got here on foot, so I'll drive you back to the Richmond Gate."

"Please help me look for Star. I can call the police, but it will probably be ages before they get here."

"Now look…" Although the Metropolitan Police Royal Parks Operational Command Unit was stationed in Holly Lodge, they knew nothing of Powell's laboratory, and Powell had no intention of risking the possibility of any of the Met's finest poking around his private domain. "What did you say your name was?"

"Dan. Daniel Nicholls. My girlfriend's name is Star Williams. She's doing some research in the park for her Master's degree. She's spoken to you before… Here's a picture of her…" Dan pulled out his smartphone and held it in front of Powell's face.

"Ah yes. Very nice girl." Powell had all but thrown the irritating bitch out of his park. She'd been snooping around, asking about missing people and throwing around some pretty wild notions. Just what he needed. Sure, people sometimes disappeared. Sure, human bones had been found on a couple of occasions. But Powell had managed to persuade everyone that they were old animal bones, and he'd disposed of them before the police could be told. He'd be damned if anything was going to interfere with the ground-breaking work he was carrying out: work that would win him a Nobel Prize, and make those Oxford bastards who'd sacked him eat their hats. "I do remember talking to her, but that was some time ago, and she definitely wasn't here today."

"Well, maybe she didn't come to see *you*. Maybe she spoke to someone else on your staff."

"I'd have known. Look, your girlfriend definitely wasn't here today. Why don't you go home; she'll probably be there already, waiting for you." Dan didn't look convinced. "There's nothing we can do now. Go home, and if your girlfriend isn't back by tomorrow morning, give me a ring and I'll talk to my staff and to the park police."

The Park Manager sounded sincere. He had a compelling way about him, and Dan started thinking that perhaps he'd overreacted. Powell picked up on his weakening resolve.

"Come on," he said. "I'll drive you to the exit."

The riders left Stag Lodge Stables and headed west towards Martin's Pond before turning north in the direction of Spankers Hill Wood.

"We're going to canter as far as those trees," the instructor told her group. "We go in single file."

There were eight of them in total. The instructor took the lead. She was a slim, athletic woman in her late twenties, her bottle blonde hair tied back in a neat ponytail just below the rim of her navy velvet riding hat. Unnoticed by all but one of the other equestrians, a silent, testosterone-fuelled shoving match briefly ensued as two dads, who were accompanying their teenage children on the hack, jostled for position directly behind the instructor. A tanned, squash-buckling stockbroker on a black gelding asserted his alpha male status, shoving a pasty, slightly overweight secondary school teacher and his mount out of the way.

"Prick!" hissed the teacher as he moved into third position behind his rival. The stockbroker grinned smugly, his eyes glued to the toned, jodhpur-clad buttocks of the riding instructor. Behind the teacher rode a meticulously-dressed woman in her forties, a hairnet keeping her hair perfect under her riding hat. A senior staff member at a management consulting firm, she paid to stable her grey mare at the Stag Lodge Stables. During the week, the stable girls exercised the mare, but she was here every weekend – rain or shine. Usually she took the mare out on her own, but the group hadn't been full, and the instructor had said she could tag along if she wanted. She'd hoped she might meet a nice man who shared her interest in horses, but the two men were oblivious to anything – including their own kids – apart from the sexy young riding instructor, and the rest of the group consisted of teenagers.

Alpha Male's daughter Harriet and her best friend from school rode behind the businesswoman. Harriet was as tanned and confident as her father, and kitted out in the latest riding gear. She rode a pretty palomino filly, whose pale mane and tail matched her own flaxen hair. Harriet's friend wore jeans rather than jodhpurs, and had borrowed a riding hat from the Stables and Harriet's old pair of riding boots, but had been riding often enough before and was happy handling her placid brown mount. The school teacher's sixteen-year-old son followed the two girls, doing his best to strike up a conversation with them while the horses were walking, but the girls ignored him – giggling and squealing like they were the only people on the ride. And then there was Freddy.

Freddy's mother had decided that the only way for him to lose weight and get some fresh air was to separate him from his geeky videogame-playing buddies and make him go riding. Team sports were out of the question, as Freddy had no athletic friends, and swimming wasn't an option as the boy absolutely refused to wear swimming trunks in public. Freddy's mum had been bringing him to Richmond

Park for riding lessons for six months now – initially in the quadrangle at the Stables, but in the past month he'd improved enough to join other riders on hacks through the park. While Freddy took part in the hour-long sessions, his mum would sit patiently in the family Volkswagen in the car park, reading the Sunday paper and listening to old songs on the car stereo.

Flaming star, don't shine on me, flaming star
Flaming star, keep behind me, flaming star
There's a lot of living I've got to do
Give me time to make a few dreams come true
Flaming star

Sometimes the rides were okay. Sometimes they were actually quite fun, especially if the other kids were friendly and if he got a decent horse. This time the hack sucked, and Freddy was already looking forward to getting home and having his friends round to play video games. He dug his heels repeatedly into his horse's flanks, but there was no way the large bay gelding with the star between its eyes was going to canter. Thick-skinned and lazy, the horse had no interest whatsoever in the chubby kid on its back. But Freddy kept kicking, and the other horses were getting further and further away, so eventually the gelding deigned to break into a trot. Freddy kept up the pressure, sweating more than his horse in an attempt to catch up with the others.

The instructor slowed her mount to a walk, then reined it in and turned to see how her group was doing. Alpha Male came to a halt right beside her. The school teacher's chestnut gelding wouldn't stop, and cantered right past the instructor, rider pulling clumsily at its reins. It finally came to an abrupt halt, the teacher narrowly avoiding falling off, and ending up wrapped around the horse's neck.

"You okay there?" the instructor enquired.

"Fine." Red-faced with embarrassment, the disgruntled teacher settled back into the saddle and reinserted his feet into the stirrups. Alpha Male smirked and tried to catch the instructor's eye. The businesswoman, the two girls and the teacher's son reigned in their mounts at the edge of the wood, and now they all stood, waiting for Freddy to catch up.

Seeing the other horses at a standstill, the bay gelding slowed from a trot to a walk again. Then it stopped, lowered its head, almost pulling the reins out of Freddy's hands, and grabbed a large mouthful of grass. Freddy dug his heels into its flanks once more, but the beast didn't even seem to notice. Freddy kicked it again, and the gelding ambled off slowly towards the waiting group, chewing as it went.

"We'll have a nice walk through the woods," the instructor said, "let the horses cool down a bit. Single file."

Freddy hadn't even caught up as the last of the group disappeared into the trees. His bum, back and legs were sore; he was tired and pissed off. Why did he always have to get the laziest, ugliest, slowest horse? He kicked the bay again, urging it on after the others.

The riders were noisy – chatting and joking as they entered the wood. Their horses rustled the bushes and snapped twigs as they made their way along the sandy track that weaved through the trees. The wind was blowing from their direction, carrying the scent of the riding party to whatever it was that watched them, unnoticed, from the leafy boughs of an ancient oak, salivating as it sucked in the musk of their sweating flesh through mud-caked nostrils.

The first seven riders moved confidently through the trees, horses striding nose to tail. The two girls were sharing a private joke, the teacher's son unable to ride up alongside them for fear of kneecapping himself on a tree. They were so far ahead of him that Freddy couldn't even see them through the trees. He let out an exasperated sigh and just sat there for a moment, one of his mother's favourite tracks going round in his head.

When I ride, I feel that flaming star
That flaming star, over my shoulder
And so I ride, front of that flaming star
Never looking around, never looking around

Mustering all his determination, Freddy pummelled the horse's flanks with his heels. No wonder cowboys wore spurs. One kick from one of those and the damn nag would be running like a racehorse. Impossibly, Freddy's horse slowed down even more, grabbing the odd mouthful of vegetation as it ambled along. As it passed under a particularly leafy old oak tree, something heavy fell on it from above. It snorted in alarm as the weight on its back suddenly increased, then disappeared altogether – the saddle being the only thing left for it to carry. Startled, it trotted a few paces after the other horses, then slowed down to a walk once more. It wasn't until the other riders had cleared the wood, the instructor stopped to regroup, and the large bay with the star wandered out riderless, that anyone noticed Freddy's disappearance.

"Oh no," the riding instructor's face dropped, and she rode up to retrieve Freddy's mount. "Would you mind holding him for me, please?" she asked Alpha Male, handing him the bay gelding's reins. She eyed the edge of the wood, expecting the chubby kid to emerge after his mount, but when he didn't, she started to worry that he might actually have hurt himself. "Could you all please wait here for me? I'll be back in five minutes." But the chubby kid was nowhere to be seen, and the panicked instructor tried to keep her voice steady as she phoned the accident through to her boss, then apologised to the group and informed them that they'd have to return to the stables immediately.

Freddy's mother looked up in surprise as she saw the group heading back after less than half an hour. Her surprise turned to despair when she spotted Freddy's riderless mount.

"Oh my God!" Mrs White scrambled out of the VW and ran towards the riders, spooking the horses in her panic. "Where's Freddy?"

"Mrs White," the instructor slid gracefully from her mount and tried to calm the woman before her shouting and arm-waving caused one of the horses to bolt. "I'm so sorry. My boss has phoned the police. They're out looking for Freddy. I'll be joining them as soon as I get the others back to the stables."

"What happened? Where's Freddy?!"

The search was in full swing. The Parks Police were directing visitors away from Spankers Hill Wood, and had cordoned off the small dark lake at its north-eastern end. A couple of officers were poking around in the muddy water with hooked poles, waiting for a Met dog unit to join them. Another officer was trying to persuade Freddy's distraught mother to go home or at least wait in her car.

"We're doing everything we can, Mrs White," soothed the officer. "If Freddy's wandered off, he might return to the car park to look for you. Why don't you go and take the weight off your feet for a bit. If there's any news, I'll come and find you. I promise."

Powell watched as the sobbing woman moved away from the policeman. She dialled a number on her mobile phone, evidently got no response, then stood and watched the police, her body language expressing utter desolation. Powell felt sorry for her, but there were far more important issues at stake. He was weeks away from creating a stem cell line closer to that of the Irish Elk than anything he'd synthesised before. He had no idea how wide the dog-led search would be. What if the animals unearthed the results of his less successful experiments? Or worse: the bones that a dog had dug up and he'd been forced to rebury after convincing the animal's owner and the less canny members of his staff present at the time that they were bovine remains and not human at all…? Perhaps the missing kid really had come to a sticky end. If it ever came out that he'd covered up a string of possible deaths in the park, he would not only lose his job and his liberty, but the Irish Elk would never walk in England's green and pleasant land again, and the name of Brendan Powell would fade into eternal insignificance. The horror.

"Mr Powell!" Powell's face fell as he turned around and saw the young man who'd lost his meddling student girlfriend. "Mr Powell, what's going on?"

Dan came to a breathless halt by the Park Manager. He hadn't been able to get hold of Powell on the phone, so he'd reported Star missing at the local police station, then headed back to the park. As Dan took in the police line and the group of officers beyond, he started to panic.

"Oh my God. Is it Star? Has something happened to Star?"

"No," sighed Powell. His day was rapidly descending into nightmare territory. "Nothing like that. A riding group lost a kid. Don't worry."

"Don't worry? What's wrong with you, man?" Dan lost his cool. He strode rapidly towards the police cordon. His determined expression attracted the attention of a police officer.

"Sir! You're not allowed in here."

"My girlfriend's missing," Dan was surprised at how shaky his voice sounded. "I thought maybe you were looking for her."

"Your girlfriend?"

As Freddy's mother, who'd been listening from a few metres away, headed towards Dan and the officer, an ashen-faced Powell headed in the opposite direction.

Like Freddy's mother, Brendan Powell hadn't slept all night. Unlike Freddy's mother, Powell had revisited the various burial sites he'd created around the back of Holly Lodge – most of them behind the building that housed the park's Met unit – going by the general rule of thumb that nobody expects crime next to a police station. He'd been lucky the previous day. The police dogs and handlers that everyone had been waiting for had been called away on account of a suspected terrorist attack in Kingston, and Powell had bought himself a night's reprieve to carry out his inspection, ready to dig up and remove anything he deemed unsatisfactorily hidden.

But his interment spots seemed secure enough, and Powell decided to let sleeping deer (and the odd human bone) lie. So with a heavy heart he burned as many cryo-samples as he could, and went to be seen to be helping the Superintendent of the Royal Parks Operational Command Unit with his search as soon as the sun came up.

Today the police dogs arrived, and led their handlers straight to a hollowed-out oak tree in Spankers Hill Wood, before setting off northwest amidst a flurry of excited yapping. Powell and the Superintendent watched them go, before returning to the Super's vehicle.

"Let me know when you find something," the Super told the dog handlers over his walkie-talkie, before turning to Freddy's bleary-eyed mother and a shattered-looking Dan, the two of whom had joined forces in their distress. "Let's all go get a cuppa, and we'll join them as soon as they have something for us."

"But I want to look for Freddy."

Officer Bennett thanked his lucky stars that, unlike the regular uniformed officers accompanying him and Briggs, he hadn't eaten breakfast that morning. He continued to stare in dismay at the two half-eaten torsos hanging above his head. The headless body was more than likely the boy who'd gone missing from the riding lesson. The other corpse was that of a young woman, her breasts and right arm missing, her belly gutted like a fish, dead eyes staring ahead, her face stained with blood, mud and tear-smeared mascara. An impossibly vibrant blue and orange star tattoo on the girl's left arm defied the dried blood and mud that caked the rest of her. Bennett hoped that the large gash on the girl's head was the indicator of a swift demise. Ozzy barked and tugged at his leash.

"Sick," Officer Briggs intoned behind Bennett like a mantra, then turned his attention back to Arnie, who was barking again and dragging his handler beneath the glossy leaves of a wild rhododendron bush. "What is it, boy?"

Bones, blood-stained clothes, three wallets, two mobile phones, a camera, a pair of glasses. Officer Briggs, the older of the two, remembered finding the odd disturbing stash of porn mags, women's underwear and sometimes even children's clothes in various London parks and commons throughout the 1980s. The presence of any clump of bushes had seemed enough reason for a pervert to set up shop. But this wasn't the lair of a regular run-of-the-mill sicko. Until recently this had been home to whoever had slaughtered the poor souls now hanging from the vast beech tree deep in the heavily timbered, fenced off section of Richmond Park known as Sidmouth Wood.

"Well done, Arnie. Come away now… Bennett, come and take a look at this."

"I've seen enough to last me a lifetime," came the response, but a moment later Bennett and Ozzy joined Briggs and Arnie under the rhododendron bush. Then the dogs were off, barking and pulling their handlers out of the bushes and through the woods.

"Make sure no one touches anything," Briggs called to the two regular officers as he reached for his walkie-talkie. The uniforms would have to wait for the Super and the crime scene investigators without him and Bennett.

"We've located two bodies in Sidmouth Wood, Sir," Briggs informed the Superintendent. "The uniforms are staying with them. We're heading west; the dogs have picked up a trail."

"I'm sorry, Mrs White, I'm afraid you'll have to stay here," the Superintendent told the distraught woman.

"But they've found something. What have they found? Have they found Freddy? Please, tell me!"

Dan approached as well, and now the Superintendent had two distressed members of the public in his face. He decided not to lie.

"They've found some human remains."

"Oh my God." Mrs White turned ashen.

"Whose remains?" asked Dan.

"We don't know that yet. If you'll excuse me, I need to get over there straight away.

"But you promised we could go with you as soon as they found something," sobbed Freddy's mother. She looked like she might collapse at any moment, and Dan comforted her; doing so distracted him from his own racing thoughts and growing nausea.

"I'm sorry, Ma'am, Sir. You need to stay here. Mr Powell will stay with you, and I'll be in constant touch with him."

Powell nodded reluctantly, desperate to know what was going on in his park, but relieved in some small way to be delaying that knowledge and the inevitable media furore that it would bring. There were already media people crawling all over the place, and Powell hoped that the police would manage to keep them away from whatever it was that the dogs had unearthed.

The shouts and baying dogs woke them from a deeper sleep than they should have allowed themselves, given that much of the girl and the remains of the chubby blond kid were still suspended in the branches of the hanging-tree, and the boy's skull and those bones that had been picked clean were still awaiting burial. Jimmy groaned awake, then yelped as his father kicked him hard in the small of his back.

"Get up, you fucking idiot! We've got to go!"

Instantly alert and attuned to the danger they found themselves in, Jimmy was up and running in seconds. He'd always known this day would come. His father had said it would. They knew what to do. The only unrehearsed part of the Doomsday Plan was the part that Jimmy was best at: work out where the potential threat was coming from, figure out which way the wind was blowing – with any luck the direction would be the same – and then flee the other way.

Jimmy had lived in the park for much of his life. His father, voted Young Conservative of the Year in 1979, had overstretched himself financially in the 1980s, gambled everything on the stock market and subsequently lost the family home and all their other worldly possessions in the crash of 1987. Wanted by his former employers, the Inland Revenue and the Serious Fraud Office for insider trading, embezzlement and a number of suspicious transactions involving hedge funds, and by the Metropolitan Police for murdering his wife who he believed was having an affair with a tax inspector, Jimmy's father had disappeared off the radar, taking his seven-year-old son with him. They lived rough, eating from bins, hiding from the police, moving from place to place. Eventually they'd ended up in Richmond Park.

Jimmy's father hardly spoke anymore, other than to bark instructions or recriminations. Without his wife's tempering influence, his aggressive streak had free reign and he'd taken to physical violence, with Jimmy bearing the brunt of his frequent rages. But he'd kept the two of them alive, stealing food from the Pembroke Lodge Cafeteria, catching ducks, fishing in the ponds, trapping small animals, and occasionally even bringing down a deer. He and Jimmy hid for much of the day and foraged for food at night.

"No one must see us!" He'd drummed the lesson into his son's head until it stuck. "You understand? If they see us, they'll kill us. Just like they killed your mother." And no one had seen them – until the day when an amateur photographer chased a shrew right into the thicket in which they'd been sleeping.

The man stopped short, staring at the filthy piles of rags lying on the ground near the spot where the shrew had disappeared into the bracken. There were feet protruding from one of the piles.

"Oh my God!" breathed the man, and next thing he knew, the larger heap of rags lifted itself from the ground and hurled itself at him. Then he was being hit over and over; the pain in his head, his face, and his arms, which he'd raised in a vain bid to protect himself, unbearable.

Jimmy merely watched as his father checked to make sure the man was dead and then wiped the man's blood from his own face.

"Get the knife," Jimmy's father grunted. Then, mistaking the surprised look in his son's eyes for disapproval, he added angrily, "Well, what are you waiting for? It's no different than the deer."

But it *was* different than the deer. It was so much better. The meat had a sweet, pungent taste to it and, when his father roasted some of it once it got dark and the park staff had left for the night, it tasted a lot like the pork that Jimmy's mum had cooked, and which he could still vaguely remember. Those memories of home, of his mother; the sweet, slightly sickly smell of the cooked meat and the glorious feeling of a full belly transformed something in Jimmy. For the first time since his life had changed so drastically, Jimmy felt a sense of well-being, of belonging, of things being as they should. He fell asleep without fear, with a new-found confidence, knowing that he was no longer the hunted – he was now the hunter.

"This way!" Jimmy shouted. The adrenaline coursing through him was urging him to fight rather than flee, and he could feel the stirrings of the erection that so often accompanied any precipitous action in his life these days, but his (infrequent) better judgement and the grim look on his father's face had him running for the western edge of Sidmouth Wood and the border of the park beyond.

"Where's the map?" Jimmy's father shouted after him.

"I've got it!" Jimmy had found the map of London tucked into the back pocket of the trousers he'd taken from a tourist he'd killed, and that's where the map had stayed, the trousers having been only slightly too big for Jimmy. The map was tattered now, but Jimmy cherished it, and it was about to play the major role in his father's D-day Plan that it had been kept for.

"You stupid fuck!" Jimmy's father shouted as he ran after him. "This is all your fault! If we get out of this alive, I'm going to kill you!"

Jimmy almost hadn't noticed the chubby blondkid on the clunky big horse – he was lagging so far behind the others. The kid was probably about his own age, and heavier than Jimmy, but Jimmy had grown large and muscular in recent months. He'd stormed off after yet another fight with his father, and the plan had been to spend a couple of hours watching the upright pigs coming and going, checking out suitable ambush sites and savouring the possibility of a kill without actually going in for one. He and his father still had much of the girl left to eat. Indeed, it was the girl who'd been the source of much of the malcontent between him and his father since Jimmy had dragged her into their main hideaway in Sidmouth Wood the previous night.

"What the fuck is this?" Jimmy's father stared at him incredulously.

"Dinner." Jimmy stood his ground.

"I've told you about this before! You're going to get us killed. They'll find us and they'll kill us, just like they killed your mother!"

"Mother was a bitch. You said so. Just like all the other bitches. Perhaps she deserved to die."

"You little shit!" Jimmy's father lashed out at him, but Jimmy was faster – he ducked his father's blow and instinctively swung at his attacker, surprising both of them when his father went down. The ill-concealed look of fear in his father's eyes gave Jimmy a rush that he hadn't felt since his first human kill. But then Jimmy saw his father's expression change from fear to panic, and followed his gaze to the spot where he'd left the sow.

"You stupid fuck!" His father had pulled himself up and pushed past Jimmy, frantically looking around the murky undergrowth. "You didn't even kill her!"

"Shit!" Jimmy dropped to all fours, studying the ground and bushes to ascertain the direction his prey had taken. He didn't need to look long. Disturbed foliage and a fresh blood trail led a short distance away to a large bush, under which Star had finally succumbed to her injuries. "It's okay. She's here."

Jimmy and his father silently dragged the body back to the thicket in which they usually processed their food. They worked swiftly, cutting off what they needed and hoisting the rest up into the hanging-tree. They lit a small fire, cooked and ate. It was Jimmy's father who finally broke the silence that had settled uncomfortably between them.

"You have to stop," he said, fully expecting another argument. But, ever the teenager, Jimmy surprised him.

"Okay." And Jimmy meant it. Until he saw the chubby blondkid alone and irresistibly vulnerable.

Jimmy hadn't counted on the fat kid being so heavy. In fact, he hadn't counted on much of anything. Nor did he have a plan on how to get back to Sidmouth Wood with the body. All he'd wanted to do was get as far away from his father as possible. Every time it was the same old story: "They'll kill us just like they killed your mother. There's enough other stuff for us to eat." But whenever Jimmy killed one of the upright pigs, his father ate it happily enough. Besides, the 'other stuff' didn't cut it with Jimmy anymore. Not only was long pig easier to procure – on account of its slowness, lack of vigilance and general stupidity, but Jimmy was completely hooked on it. It was hard to tell which excited him more: the exhilaration of the hunt, the thrill of the kill, the sweet taste of the meat or the sense of wellbeing that the eating brought. Jimmy started to get aroused again just thinking of the moment when he leapt on the fat kid's back. He'd brought him off his horse, twisted his neck and pulled him into the undergrowth without a moment's hesitation. It was a single, flowing movement – an action so perfect that it must have been rehearsed over and over somewhere in Jimmy's collective unconscious and woven into the very fabric of his DNA.

But once he'd made the kill, Jimmy realised that he needed to get out fast. Even with a much lighter body it wouldn't have been possible as there was a lack of tree cover between Spankers Hill Wood and the larger Sidmouth Wood, too many people and too many hours of daylight still left. And then he heard one of the riders returning. With a supreme effort, Jimmy dragged the remains into the hollowed-out trunk of an ancient tree. He pulled a vast piece of peeled bark over the hollow, and determined to stay there with the corpse until dark. Unbeknown to him, his luck was in. The same incident that bought the Park Manager time by keeping the Met's dog unit away also ensured that Jimmy's hiding-place went undetected for the rest of the day. Once night fell, he returned to Sidmouth Wood to apologise to his father and ask for his help, and the two of them dragged Freddy's remains back to their lair in time for an early meal.

They broke cover and headed west by north west, just as the police dogs and officers entered the wood from the opposite direction. The dead bodies distracted their pursuers long enough to give them the chance to get clear of Sidmouth Wood and, as Ozzy and Arnie picked up their scent, they were already heading for Petersham Gate and out of the park.

They crossed Petersham Road, and darted into the alleyway directly ahead. The narrow footpath weaved between large suburban houses, and father and son followed it, emerging by the little graveyard behind St Peter's Church. Jimmy's father had lived on Richmond Hill, frequently strolling around Petersham Meadows and the surrounding area, so he quickly got his bearings. They turned right at the church, then left past Petersham Nurseries, along another footpath. A bricked-up arch loomed on their right. They hurried on, turning right onto River Lane, past Petersham Lodge and through Petersham Woods, finally reaching the Thames.

The river stretched grey before them; Glover's Island to their right. It was a cold, rainy day, and the path along the river was mercifully devoid of human presence. The only immediate causes of concern were the houseboats bobbing on the dark water and the distant sound of police sirens. Jimmy's father studied the boats closely. To their left, on the far side of the river, just visible in the bushes, was a small, grubby boat, an outboard motor attached to the stern. Who'd leave an engine attached to a boat? That was asking for trouble. Perhaps it wasn't working, or the owner of the boat was close by. But if there was even the slightest possibility that the motor was functional, then the risk of finding out was worth it.

"Listen, you stupid shit," Jimmy's father was breathing heavily from the exertion of their escape, "we'll go right down to the water and head downriver for a bit, as far as the island. That way they'll think we crossed there and they'll look for us on the island or the far bank. But we'll double back along our tracks from our starting point on the bank – there – and swim across to that boat – over there. If we can get the motor started, we'll head upriver – there. If not, we'll take a houseboat. But we'll have to move fast so the owners won't have time to make a sound." Jimmy grinned in response. His father glowered at him, adding, "We try the boat first. Let's go!"

They were lucky. The engine started and they were soon heading upriver: southwest, past Eel Pie Island, then south past Twickenham and Teddington. A police helicopter flew overhead, but didn't spot them or raise the alarm. The pilot headed straight for the southern bank of the Thames opposite Glover's island, where Ozzy and Arnie were running frantically back and forth.

The river looped west, then north, around the Hampton Court Grounds. As Brendan Powell sat facing Freddy's sobbing mother and a scowling, morose Dan in Richmond Park's Met Unit base, Jimmy and his father passed Tagg's Island unnoticed and disembarked in the bushes by St Alban's Riverside Walk. They removed the motor from the boat and hid it in a fenced-off section of undergrowth near a small weir. Then they sank the boat itself and crossed Hampton Court Road, slipping into their new home via the Hampton Gate…

So this park wasn't as big as the one they'd been living in. So there wouldn't be as many animals to eat. But in a city boasting over fifteen million tourists a year, one particular type of hairless animal would never be in short supply. And the river air had done wonders for Jimmy's appetite.

Bushy Park. The second largest of England's Royal Parks. 1099 acres of woodlands, grassland, gardens and ponds. Home to 320 deer, 150 types of solitary bees and wasps, 123 species of endangered invertebrates, an undisclosed number of metre-long carp and… something else.

The High Priestess

Dan Coxon

Heathen

They're on holiday when he sees the cottage. Julie and Nico are bickering in the back seat, Maggie searching through the glovebox for something – anything – that might shut them up for five minutes. He rubbernecks as they pass it at speed, pulls into a lane half a mile up the road.

"What are you stopping for?" Maggie asks, feeding an audiobook into the stereo.

"Nothing. Just want to check something out," Rob replies.

He almost misses the cottage again, but the For Sale sign peeks above the dry-stone wall just in time, alerting him to hit the brakes. There's a gravel layby for parking, so he pulls into it and kills the engine. The building is only small, walls of piled stone, a thatched roof that looks mouldy in places, sticking up in tufts like a hairstyle gone wrong. The front door is painted white, worn away to the bare wood in patches. There's a large garden at the rear, sweeping away from the road and partway up the hill behind it. He thinks he sees a path and a gate. A trail leads up the slope.

"Won't be a moment," he says, stepping out of the car. Maggie shouts something, but he can't tell if it's aimed at him or the children.

Peering through the window, Rob can see the cottage is deserted. He has to bend to press his nose to the glass, his eyes adjusting to reveal an empty room. Cracked tiles on the floor, a thick layer of dust forming a minimalist carpet.

It gives him permission to climb over the waist-high gate to one side, into the rear garden. The grass is patchy and weeds have pushed through the lawn but the path is still there, leading to another gate at the far end, becoming a dirt track that ascends the hill. He can't see the top, but he assumes it stretches all the way to the crest. There's something fascinating about that hill. The way it swells from the flat land around it, the pleasing curve of its rise and fall. He stands and stares at it for a minute, thinking.

When he returns to the car Nico has fallen asleep in his seat, while Julie is munching her way through a giant packet of Wotsits, the orange dust smeared across her face like pollen. Maggie's look dares him to comment on her parenting choices.

As he clicks his seat belt into place and restarts the engine, he says, "I like this place. Mind if we swing by the estate agents in town? Just to see how much it's going for."

The asking price is a fraction of their home's value. Once the holiday has passed they spend several evenings arguing over it, but he gets his way in the end. They can buy it with the equity, live there mortgage-free. He can work remotely, while Maggie's online business can be managed from anywhere with a Wi-Fi signal. The children will have to change schools, but that might be for the better; the countryside is a healthier place to grow up than the bustle and fumes of the city. It's a pleasant surprise to discover that the deeds include the hill too, a plot of land that stretches to the brook running behind it. The kids can play there, build a fort in the apple tree. Most importantly, they can all breathe again. In the countryside they will meet their true selves.

They move into the cottage two months later. The children complain that it smells weird, and Maggie finds fault on a daily basis, from the rusted plumbing to the inch-high gap at the bottom of the door that lets in an occasional mouse, but Rob is happy. While they bicker and unpack boxes, lining the new nest, he stands in the garden and stares up at the hill.

Maggie finds a handyman in the village. It's what she does, managing the cottage as she would her business. A young man with a wild thicket of brown hair and a warm smile – Derek – who fits a new door and tidies up the thatch. She spends hours making him cups of tea and guiding him from job to job, fixing and replacing, turning this pile of stones into a home. She doesn't mind too much when he walks mud across the living room floor, or when he knocks his tea over, staining the stairs brown. "You can't make an omelette," she says. "And so on."

While Derek's fixing up their home, Rob spends most of his time in the garden. It's quiet, away from the banging hammers and the boiling kettle. The Wi-Fi coverage is patchy, and his laptop won't connect when he sits on the bench by the apple tree. Instead, he rests it on his lap and pretends to work. His eyes follow the line of the path, straight as an arrow, up the hillside to the sky.

One day he leaves his laptop on the bench and walks to the gate at the back of the lawn. The path up the hill is steep and the stones are loose, forcing him to scrabble on hands and knees. He wipes the mud on his V-neck jumper. The trail fades in and out of existence as he nears the top, like someone's dream of a path that used to be there, or a premonition of what is to come, but he does not slow down and he always finds his way again.

When he reaches the top – finally, his thighs burning, his trousers dirty and torn – he discovers it is flat, a level platform of scrubby grass and stones. Turning, he can see for miles in every direction. He sits and hums to himself, waiting for whatever comes next.

The Awakening

It's hard to say whether he dreams the stairs, or if they simply come to him one afternoon as his fingers claw at the tufts of grass. He has taken to climbing the hill several times a day, sitting at the top for an hour or more. It clears his mind. The experience is the closest he has come to something spiritual. He does not say the word 'God', not even to himself, but the concept nestles in his thoughts.

The sketch he draws for Derek is simplistic and out of scale, like something his children might draw. It does not reflect the impressive structure he envisions but it is the best he can manage.

"So it's a stair?" Derek says, having turned it this way and that, holding it up against the sunlight pouring through the window.

"Yes," Rob replies, his finger pointing to the pencil lines. "A staircase. All the way up the hill, from our gate to the top. Straight, like the path."

Derek looks at him, then back to the drawing.

"I could do it, I guess. That's a lot of wood, though. And a lot of work. I might need to hire another couple of pairs of hands, plus a bigger van… Are you sure? It won't be cheap."

Rob is sure. He's never been more certain of anything in his life.

Maggie takes some convincing. The work won't even make a dent in their savings – Rob was a hot-shot in derivatives, back when he wanted to be – but it's the principle of the thing that matters. They shouldn't be throwing away money on a vanity project, a frivolous set of steps that lead nowhere in particular. Can't he just buy some better boots?

It's not about the climb, though, or the view from the crest of the hill. Rob can't quite explain it, not even to himself, but there's a greater plan at work here. He has faith that someday it will all make sense.

Once they've approved the job, Derek sets to work. He thinks it's an enormous waste of his time. He tries to find the most durable materials, but even using those he doubts the staircase will last more than ten years, maybe fifteen.

The posts will rot in the ground, the winter winds will tear it away in strips. But he's learned over the years that it isn't his role to offer advice, or marriage counselling. His place is to work the wood and make something new, so that is what he does. That he does it rather well does not go unnoticed by Rob, or by Maggie.

It takes Derek and his team – a boy in his teens called Mikey, and an overweight older man who goes by the name 'Hutch'– almost two months to complete the stairs. There's some debate over whether planning permission is required, but since the structure is on private land nothing is ever done about it. Rob knows his money will smooth things over if it has to. The important thing is that the stairs are built, and as close to his sketch as possible. It's like magic, watching that childish drawing manifest on the hillside in actual wood and nails. Despite the cheap oak finish and a few steps that don't quite sit straight, it's a sight to behold, that stairway ascending the side of the hill. Like a pathway to something better.

They walk up it that evening. All four of them, as a family. Julie and Nico call a ceasefire for a few minutes, and they stand atop the hill, holding hands, staring out at the view.

"I guess that doesn't suck," Julie says. It's possibly the most enthusiasm she's ever shown for anything.

After a couple of minutes the kids get bored, and Maggie uses them as an excuse to walk back down to the house and make herself a pot of tea. Rob stays behind. Looking around him, he feels something swell in his chest, like a balloon expanding inside his ribcage.

It's at this moment that he hears the voice.

He isn't sure that it's a voice at all, not at first. There's a rustle of leaves that lasts a little too long, a babble from the brook that almost suggests something more. The wind blows harder than before, *hush*ing past his ear.

Then a word, as clear as if someone were standing behind him.

Build.

Rob turns to see who's there, and when there's nobody within sight he assumes he was simply mistaken. Sound can play funny tricks if you're not careful. But there it is again, coming from in front of him this time, where there's *definitely* nobody to be seen.

Build.

When he talks back he feels rather foolish, standing on a hill by himself in the middle of the countryside, holding conversation with someone he cannot see.

"Build what?" he asks. Then again: "What should I build?"

Church, the voice says. Or it may have been *Temple* – somehow it says both at once, as if the word and the concept are one and the same.

Rob has questions. Many of them are about the voice itself, and where it comes from, but most are about the temple he wants to build. He recognises that now. Not just the instruction, but the desire to build a church on this hill, where it can be seen for miles around. He feels that he has a purpose at last.

When he returns to the garden almost an hour later he can hear Derek and Maggie laughing in the kitchen, but he doesn't join them. Instead, he reaches for his pencil and pad, and he begins to sketch.

Ex nihilo

Construction is slow at first. Rob knows nothing about buildings, and it turns out that Derek doesn't either. Hutch has a cousin who used to be an architect, and they throw enough money his way that he's happy to turn Rob's sketches into something like a plan. After a month of late-night phone calls and emails querying what this or that squiggle means, they have an official blueprint, with dimensions, and visualisations, and cutaway illustrations. When he looks at it, Rob sees the building the voice described to him.

Officially they're meant to submit the plans to the local council for approval, but Rob says not to worry, it's all taken care of. Derek wonders exactly what is taken care of, and how, but he keeps his mouth shut. He's being paid more than he's earned in a lifetime of odd jobs and window cleaning, and his mother always taught him not to look a gift horse in the mouth. He doesn't have enough of an education to know the other sayings about gift horses and Greeks.

The foundations are the toughest part. With his limited knowledge of building techniques, Derek has to spend a couple of days watching videos on YouTube. It looks simple enough, but when they come to break ground – Rob treating them all to a glass of bubbly grape juice and Belinda Carlisle's 'Heaven is a Place on Earth' – they find that the soil is thick with stones, some the size of a grown man's fist. Getting the digger up the hillside was bad enough, but now it struggles to scoop more than half a bucket at a time, the metal screaming against tumours of flint.

When the time comes for the pour, they bring in as many hands from the village as they can. Some have previous construction experience, but others – Jim who works in the butchers, Silas from the Laughing Lady – are there purely to add muscle. Derek directs them as best he can, standing to one side in his brand new Barbour jacket and wellies. The community spirit spills over into the back room of the Laughing Lady until the following morning, and they have to delay the next stage of building by a day. Rob acts annoyed, but he doesn't care. When he looks at the concrete platform they have made he sees only what it will become.

The frame goes up next, a timber skeleton like the hull of an upturned ship. Derek is on more familiar ground now they're down to planks and joists, and he occasionally rolls up his jacket sleeves and lends a hand. The wood is delivered on the back of a flatbed truck that can barely make it around the twists and turns of the access road, then they have to carry it up the steps one piece at a time. It's almost Biblical, seeing all those bare-chested men hauling crossbeams up the hill. When they're done, it sits in a shambolic pile to one side of the foundations, like a child's construction set ready to be assembled, or a bonfire waiting to be lit. They cover it with two brand-new tarps, but the rain doesn't come.

As they work, hauling the pillars upright and setting them in the ground, sawing the angles for the rafters, Rob sprawls on the grass and watches. He has abandoned his laptop for good – his employers fired him after half a dozen disciplinary cases for non-attendance, and he accepted their settlement payout with open arms. In this place they have more than enough money to last them until the end of their lives. He has no need of any more.

He takes to sleeping in the open body of the church, drifting off with the dome of the heavens above him. It's cold, but he has an inner fire that warms him. He knows that something will happen here – he just doesn't know when, or what. They are building something truly great but the miracle is yet to come. The voice still speaks to him from time to time, usually in the middle of the night, when he's unsure whether he's awake or asleep. It has found its voice now – a woman's, resonant and clear – and it speaks in full sentences rather than single words. They are bringing it to life with their labour.

This is my house and you shall build it for me, it says.

With your hands you will build life everlasting, it says.

Inside these walls you pledge yourself to me, it says.

Rob always smiles when he hears its words, and when he sleeps he dreams of a great cavernous hall, thronged with people, their voices swelling to the heavens.

Once the framework is completed the walls go in. They are of a unique design, two layers of plasterboard with straw packed in between. Rob thinks he saw something similar in a magazine once, but the design came from the voice, not from him. The straw will insulate the church, he imagines. Keep them all warm inside.

"…and the first pig built his house of straw…" Derek mutters as the men wrestle armfuls of it into the cavities, but Rob pretends not to hear. Derek's role has largely become an honorary one, he's only occasionally on site to supervise. Rob wants to see them breathe life into this temple first-hand.

Finally the doors and windows are fitted, the exterior is painted in brilliant white, and they stand back to admire what they have done. Tomorrow the pews will arrive – pitch-pine, hand carved – and the six-foot-wide slab of oak trunk that will serve as their altar. There are candles too, and oil lamps, and twenty bottles of paraffin to fuel them. Thick velour curtains, in bright red and green, to hang along the walls.

The time is almost here.

Bethel

Maggie breaks the news to him after dinner one night, the children tucked safely into bed.

"I never meant for this to happen," she says, a wine glass clutched in both hands as if she intends to bludgeon him with it. "Neither of us did. But you're never here any more, and Derek… well, he's been here with me. *For* me. The only future I can see is a future with him."

Rob knows he should ask whether she loves him, but he finds that he honestly doesn't care. All his thoughts are of the church, and the voice in his head. It speaks to him day and night, awake and asleep; it tells him that he is doing something truly incredible, that the day will soon come when it will reveal itself and their world will change forever.

"Okay," he says, uncertain of what else is expected. "What will we tell the kids?"

"Julie and Nico already know," Maggie says. "They've moved all their toys to Derek's house, we're going to live there. He has a hot tub and a fifty-inch TV. His Wi-Fi is excellent."

Rob nods. "As long as you still have time to help with the posters," he says.

He's been working on the posters for the past two weeks, during the final stages of the construction. It was important that he got the wording just right. He wants as many people as possible to be there for the grand unveiling. *Fill my church from wall to wall*, the voice tells him, and he desires nothing more than to please her.

The printers are due to deliver them tomorrow, then he has a team lined up to distribute them through the local villages. This is too big to keep to their local circle. The posters range from shop-window A4 to 48-sheet billboards, the words shining from them in orange and red: *Grand unveiling. Experience our new Church in all its majesty. A Special night of Celebration and Miracles. All welcome. Bring your Families!* The time and location are at the bottom, but he knows they will find it easily enough. Now that it's painted, the building stands on their hill like a beacon, a lighthouse for the lost and the abandoned. There's an artist's impression of it on the poster, too. Rob had tried to sketch it himself, but he'd finally had to admit that his artistic skills weren't up to the job; as it turned out, Jim the butcher was surprisingly proficient with a set of charcoals.

Rob sits on the hill the following evening and watches the lights twinkling in far-off villages, the orange bubbles of the street lights. He knows which posters have gone where; there are two billboards by the glowing disc of the roundabout, five on bus stops along the main road through town. Looking out, he imagines each tiny light is someone's soul, sparked into life by the opportunity he is giving them.

You must fill our hall, the voice says, nearby, as if talking over his shoulder. *Bring them all into the light.*

She's been saying that – or something similar – for the last twenty-four hours, and it's getting a little tiresome, if he's honest. Still, as he turns and looks at the brilliant white façade of the church, his heart fills, and he cannot wait for them to come and see what he has built. If he is proud, he tells himself, then it is only the pride of the shepherd who is saving his flock. What he is saving them for never crosses his mind.

On the night itself he wears a new suit, bought especially for the occasion: white blazer, white trousers, even white shoes. He is '68 Comeback Special Elvis, and he feels that he might ignite with joy. He stands at the doors to the church and watches the stream of believers as they gather candles from the bucket at the foot of the steps, lighting them as they head up the stairway, a river of flame in the dark. Quietly he hums George Michael's 'Faith' and tries to brush pink stains from his jacket sleeves. There are those he knows – Hutch, his cousin the architect, young Mikey – with their families and loved ones, but also faces he has never seen before, drawn to the light on top of the hill. They chatter and buzz, taking their places in the pews, and their excitement is infectious. Maggie and the kids are sitting in the front row, and Nico has started jumping up and down, unable to contain his enthusiasm, almost setting his little waistcoat alight with his candle. Derek sits with them, and Rob is glad. It's good that they have found some happiness, when everything in this world is so fleeting.

Once the pews are filled to capacity, the pine creaking and warping beneath so many well-fed backsides, he directs people to stand in the aisles, under the windows, even around the oakwood altar. They push up against each other, shoulder to shoulder, until he cannot imagine anyone else squeezing in. Then he signals to Jim the butcher to close the doors, and he begins to make his way forward. He jostles where he has to, asks forgiveness as he pushes people aside. It's a slow crawl through a sea of bodies to reach the front, but once he's there he moves around the island of the altar, grips the rough bark of its edge.

You have filled my house, the voice says, so close now that it might be inside his head. *You have brought these people to witness the light. Now it is time.*

He smiles.

The High Priestess

Nobody is sure when she first appears, or how. She is not there, and then she is, as if she has always been. If Rob is disappointed that she doesn't arrive with a fanfare and a choir of angels, then he keeps that to himself. This, surely, is miracle enough.

The crowd stares at first. This is not what anyone expected, not what they had signed up to witness. But in truth, none of them know what they have signed up for. Only that they were called and they came here, to witness something incredible.

If the way she materialises from nothing does not fulfil that expectation, then her appearance surely does.

She is shorter than any of the adults, closer to Julie's height, but she makes up for it by floating two feet off the ground. Her form was once human, but it has moved beyond that, disassembling and renewing like a corpse in the soil, playing host to other creatures as they're drawn to her warmth. Her ribs are a cage, the bird that flutters within them nothing more than feathers and skin; as they watch, a millipede the length and width of a man's belt skitters from where her ear should be and wraps itself around her neck. Her face is constantly changing, rotting away then blooming back to health, a ruddy-cheeked girl one second, an emaciated hag the next. Her fingers, when she holds out her hands, are long and knotted like twigs.

Welcome to my house, she says. *My children.*

The screaming starts at the front and spreads through the congregation like crashing waves. Rob signals to Jim at the back, and he fits the bar across the doors. This was expected. There are always those who fear the miracle when it comes.

She had told him this, several days before. She had lain with him on the concrete floor of the church, his hand tied up in the twisted vines of her hair, her stiff, cold fingers between his legs.

They will not understand, she said, her voice like the gurgling of the brook, or the wind in the grass. *They have never seen the world as it truly is, and now that their eyes are opened, they will cry and tear at their breasts. This has happened before and it shall happen again.*

"But then they'll find the joy, right?" he asked, the words catching in his throat. "Once they understand, when they see you, won't they be filled with wonder? Just your existence, it's… a miracle. Magical. How could they not kneel down and worship you when they see what you truly are?"

There was a sound that may have been a sigh, or simply her skin crackling like fallen leaves.

You have seen me and your eyes have been opened. You have beheld my true form and not turned mad. Is it too much to hope they may do the same?

Rob isn't so sure about that, although he doesn't give voice to his doubts. Part of him wonders if he has, indeed, gone mad. The things he has seen should never have appeared before mortal eyes. And yet something led him along the path to this point – to the cottage, and the hill, and the steps, and the church – and now that he's here he cannot imagine anywhere else that he could possibly be.

He ponders on this as the people begin to hammer on the door and the walls, their screams turning to anger and tears. As her birds take flight and peck out their eyes.

Cupio dissolve

He tells himself that this was always the plan. It's comforting to know that he's fulfilled something, that he's ticked that box and can move on. Rob has always been very goal-oriented. Even as he watches Maggie scream and clutch at her face, blood oozing between her fingers as she staggers blindly about the gathering; even as young Mikey gags on the millipede that comes crawling out of his mouth, its mandibles shining and slick. Rob feels something like pride as he takes a deep breath, smells the tang of their fear, the sweat and adrenaline. And the paraffin.

Ah, yes. The paraffin.

When she'd first told him he'd balked at the idea. After all, this church was his masterwork, the project that finally put him on the map. It was a temple to her greatness, yes, but wasn't it also a monument to his achievements? Hadn't she led him here to create this beacon?

She had made a clicking noise in the back of her throat, like teeth gnashing at air. Shifting her body, she had twisted and writhed until she lay on top of him, the stink of rot sweet and earthy in his nostrils.

Everything must end, she had said, her words spoken slowly and clearly. It was important that he understood. *There is no eternity, there is no forever. That is man's vanity. Your meaning lies in your ending, and we shall give them an ending to be proud of. We will give them an ending that will be talked about for centuries, and then they will be reborn when their ashes feed new life. That is the best anyone can dream of.*

She was right, of course. He could see that now. Beyond the stink of piss and freshly spilled blood, he could smell them for what they truly were: cattle, animals destined for the slaughter. The pig doesn't self-visualise as a bacon sandwich, does it? Well, then.

It had taken him most of the night to drill the holes in the plasterboard, then to pour the paraffin in, one bottle at a time. It was only an accelerant, of course. The straw would act as kindling, the timber frame would burn for hours. This had all been built into the church from the start. This was all part of the plan.

If he has a regret as he takes the lighter from his pocket and holds it to the curtains – velour, the best wick money can buy – it's that it will all be over so soon. He's done something truly magical here, hasn't he? Who can say they have done anything even half as great? But he knows it's all in how you make your exit. And as his goddess sings her victory, and the aisles flow with blood, the flames begin to crawl up the walls, searching with their tongues until they find the paraffin within and burst into sudden, brilliant light.

The Hierophant

Jonathan Sims

Education. Convention. Tradition.

To call it a hidden door would not have been accurate. If anything, it did everything in its power to call attention to itself, dominating as it did the whole back wall of the professor's office. But if Nick had been asked to tell you which part of the ornate wooden design was the actual *door*, to point to the lines where it joined with the surrounding mass of darkly-stained ash wood, he could not have done so. It was a colossal thing, partly a pair of bookshelves covered with weighty and austere looking tomes, and partly an intricate carving of scenes and figures that Nick had never been able to fully place. They implied the shape of bearded men hunched over books and stern, knowledgeable lords sat in seats of judgement. Over the top of what Nick was *almost* certain would have been the middle of the door was a shape that he thought probably represented King Solomon but, as with so much else when he sat in that office, he simply wasn't certain.

This uncertainty, unfortunately, also included his studies. No matter how much he worked on his essays, or how many hours he spent slaving over history books and sitting in droning lectures, it made no difference once he sat in that hard wooden chair. His perfectly sourced and well-articulated arguments seemed suddenly shallow and foolish. Professor Hughes had only to slightly tilt his head to the side or curl his mouth into something that might just have been a condescending smile, and all at once Nick would become painfully aware of his accent, of how the Birmingham drawl felt like it rendered his sentences absurd. The shapes of words he had happily spoken his whole life seemed now to hang in his mouth, twisting it into all sorts of strange self-conscious configurations. It didn't help that the professor seemed to delight in setting topics which always seemed to require Nick to struggle through Latin or Greek terms that he didn't have the first idea of how to pronounce.

And throughout it all, that doorway loomed in the back. Its strange and judgemental figures staring out from the frame with lifeless wooden eyes. They had their opinions of his academic work as well, it seemed, and they were no more favourable than his tutor's.

'Well,' Professor Hughes said, as he did every time Nick finished reading his essays, 'that was a fascinating perspective, Nicholas. Thank you for sharing.'

He turned his attention away from Nick then (a dismissal so polite that surely it couldn't be as hurtful as it felt?) and focused his attention on Nick's tutorial partner. George Granville was tall, broad and blonde, his rowing-team shoulders always seeming to be on the verge of breaking through his expensive Ralph Lauren polo shirts. He stood up straight, and never appeared to struggle with finding a comfortable way to sit on the chairs in the professor's office. Nick sometimes secretly suspected that George's chair was more comfortable than his, but of course that was nonsense. Both chairs looked exactly the same.

Everything about George was more comfortable in this office. He sat there like it was his absolute right, and as much as Nick might have despised him for his rich upbringing and bone-deep sense of entitlement, he couldn't disagree that, of the two of them, George was the one this room was built for. And as his tutorial partner began to read out his own essay, the words and antiquated terminology tripping easily from his lips, it could hardly be denied that it sounded that way as well. George's clipped, plummy accent ("The Queen's English", Nick's dad would have called it) seemed to wrap its way around the argument he was making, lending it an air of authority and expertise. Nick never had any idea what his partner was actually talking about in his essays. Half the time it seemed almost like nonsense and, indeed, his limited interactions with the man outside of their tutorials painted him as not much of a scholar, but when he spoke the words no longer seemed to matter. It was so clear that of course he knew what he was talking about. Why else would Professor Hughes spend the whole time nodding?

The tutorial ended the way it always did, with the professor discussing George's essay in detail, giving feedback and pointing out insights in his quiet, precise voice, then thanking them both for their time and gesturing for them to leave.

George rose immediately, but Nick lingered for a moment, waiting to see if Professor Hughes would use the door at the back of the office. He had only ever done so once before, during the second ever tutorial they had had together, and Nick had gotten the briefest of glimpses inside. It had been a larger room of some sort, full of books and leather armchairs and hushed, learned conversation. There had been others there: pale faces with bristling white hair and expressions that spoke of sober study and comfort. It had lasted only a moment before the door had closed again behind the professor, but since then it had plagued Nick's mind. He was desperate to see it again, as though to see it might give him some insight into how he might gain access, how he might join those who deserved to be there.

'Can I help you, Mr Davis?' the professor asked, and Nick realised he was still sitting in place.

'Uh, no, thank you,' he started to rise to his feet.

'See you next week.' There was something in Professor Hughes' voice that seemed sharper than usual.

'Yeah. You too.'

And then Nick was out the door and away. The professor watched him depart, waiting until he was gone before dropping his face back into a sneer. He got up and walked over to the chair he kept specially for the poor lad and looked it over. He shook his head slowly, the look of disgust only leaving his face when he noticed a few tiny drops of blood where Nick's hands had gripped the seat. Then the sneer was replaced with a smile.

"So you're doing ok then?"

His father seemed to sound older every time Nick phoned up. He remembered how strange it had been over the Christmas break, to see the man he remembered as strong and proud struggling to carry a suitcase.

"Yeah," Nick felt like he was lying, even though his marks had been fine. "It's a lot of work, you know."

"Well, that's why they let you in," his dad said proudly. "Because of how hard you work. They know a future scholar when they see one!"

"I guess. It just feels like not everyone here has to work as hard as I do."

"Ignore them. They're just rich little shits who got in because their grandfather's a duke or something. They don't deserve to be there any more than you do."

"It's not that bad."

"No? What about that guy you telling me about last week? In your class?"

"George. And it's not a class, it's a tutorial."

"What's the difference?"

"There's a bunch of you in a class," Nick explained for what felt like the tenth time, "a tutorial's just two of you and the tutor. You read your essays and talk about them."

"Hm. Guess they do it weird at posh unis," his dad said. "Still, don't let them convince you they're any better than you are. It's all an act."

"Doesn't feel like it sometimes."

"Just remember: you had to fight to be where you are right now. You deserve to be there more than any of them."

"Sure thing dad. Anyway, I've got to go. I've got reading to do."

"Alright, lad. Talk soon."

Nick put the phone down and sighed. It wasn't that his father was wrong, exactly. He was the only one from his comprehensive school that had managed to get a place at the most prestigious university in the country, maybe even the world. He'd struggled through schools, teachers and classmates that had all relentlessly told him he'd never make it and he had proved them wrong. But in many ways it didn't matter. It wasn't really about deserving. The longer he spent here, the more he tried to throw himself into the place, academically and socially, the more he started to realise that this place simply wasn't *for* him. Without money and without the breezy confidence of one who had never truly had to earn anything, he didn't feel like he had a place here. He didn't even understand what other people were talking about half the time, sharing anecdotes about travelling in France or annual ski trips while he sat there trying to think whether he should tell the story of the Summer they spent playing every day in the community park because their electricity had been cut off. It was a different world, and it didn't seem to want him.

At least, most of the time. There were moments, just occasionally, when he would catch people staring at him. Lecturers, tutors, occasionally even other students, when they thought he couldn't see them. It was hard to exactly pin down the expression on their faces, but the closest thing would probably be hunger.

The day of his next tutorial, Nick woke early, starting up from a vivid nightmare where a stern-looking priest gazed down indifferently from a great throne as his death sentence was uttered. He had trespassed in the holy man's court, and in punishment was to be flayed alive, with his skin cured and used to bind books of wisdom. The knife came quickly, and Nick woke just as it started to bite into his flesh.

When he finally emerged, clawing and gasping from the hands of the dream, he lay there in the darkness for several moments, the sweat cooling on his still-intact skin. The sheets were soaked through, and while his phone said it was still only 4:37, he knew he wasn't going to be getting back to sleep. Instead he turned on the light and flicked the switch on a small travel kettle his father had given him for his room as a going-away present. He stumbled over to his desk, where his laptop stood open, ready for him to resume work.

And he was just about to do exactly that, when a faint noise reached his ears. Something had moved, not within his room, but just outside. It was almost nothing, and if his senses had not been wired from his rude awakening Nick would never have noticed it, but there had been a definite sound of shifting weight from just outside the door to his room. He stopped, a sense of dread settling in his stomach that he couldn't quite rationalise, and he reached over the desk, flicking off the lamp that had been illuminating the place.

The room was once again dark, but the corridors of his halls of residence were always lit, and sure enough, the thin sliver of light at the base of his doorway was broken by the distinct shadows of a pair of shoes. This fact had barely registered when they moved, disappearing from their spot outside and moving quickly away, accompanied by the soft but unmistakable sound of footsteps along the carpeted hall.

By the time Nick had got the door open, the corridor was empty, and there was no sign that anyone had been there at all. He went back to the desk, his legs ever so slightly shaking. Why was he so on edge about someone walking through the building? Obviously someone passing by had heard him wake up violently and stopped to listen in case he needed help. He was quite literally jumping at shadows.

Nick turned the light back on and pressed a button on his laptop. The screen immediately sprang to life with his as-yet-unfinished next essay. He sighed and rubbed his face, trying to massage some wakefulness into it. His hand came away bloody. Another nosebleed? He reached for a tissue, wondering not for the first time why he'd started getting them so often since he arrived here. It must be something in the air.

The next tutorial was even worse than Nick had expected. He was exhausted, still feeling the effects of his nightmare-sponsored lack of sleep. Even more than that, his whole body seemed so weak that just walking up the stairs to Professor Hughes' office felt like an endurance test. He was worried he might be coming down with something, but there were no symptoms other than this bone-deep fatigue and these persistent nosebleeds. Neither of which would have been considered acceptable excuses for not attending his tutorial.

He slumped down in the chair, his body expecting some respite, but was met by only the agonising discomfort of the wooden seat. It dug into his limbs, forcing his back almost completely straight, but not quite allowing his shoulders to do the same. Nick was sure he must have made some grunting noise of pain, but if George or the professor noticed it, they did not react. Behind the soft, plush-looking fabric of Hughes' armchair, the carved wooden door stood silent. Had it been polished since last he had seen it? The woodstain seemed darker, somehow, and shinier. The eyes of the carved figures gleamed as they stared blankly out at him. He wanted so desperately to see it open again, to go through it.

It was only at that point that Nick realised he had started speaking. He was already reading his essay, dimly aware of how clumsy his phrasing seemed, how inane his insights probably were, how ridiculous it all sounded coming out of his mouth. He wanted to stop, to get up and run from the smirking assessment of Hughes and George, but he kept talking anyway. Then he reached the end of the essay and the sound of his own voice ceased.

"Well," said Professor Hughes, "quite."

That was it? That was *it?* All he had to say, all the feedback to the days of effort Nick had poured into his writing.

"Do you, uh…" Nick's voice stumbled slightly. "Do you have any more specific feedback you'd like to discuss?"

Professor Hughes smiled beneficently.

"I'm sure it was excellent," he smirked. "I just sometimes have trouble following your, um, accent, I'm afraid."

There should have been anger igniting in Nick's heart, there should have been fury. But there was only blank grey fatigue. He watched as George coughed politely to hide his nasty little chuckle, before theatrically pulling out his own sheets of closely-typed A4 paper. As he gathered them together and began to say something about approaches to Historiography, Nick caught a glimpse of the words printed right at the start of George's essay: *Lorem ipsum dolor sit amet.*

Hang on, was that placeholder text? George hadn't written a damn thing. He was just making it up as he went along! Nick's eyes flicked over to the professor, expecting to see the shadow of irritation at the obvious bullshit being spouted as if it was academia. But there was nothing in Hughes' face but approval. After all, it did sound like a well-written essay. In fact, wait, was that a phrase from *his* essay? No, of course not, he couldn't simply parrot Nick's essay at a person who had literally just heard it. It was so familiar, though, and coming out of George's mouth it sounded erudite and incisive, not ignorant or awkward at all.

Either way, Nick was in no fit state to raise any sort of objection, and all he could do was stare blankly at his partner. He was aware, faintly, of the *drip drip drip* of another nosebleed, but for the life of him he couldn't see where the blood was going.

At last it was over, and Professor Hughes stood up.

"Excellent work today, George," his voice hinted at satisfaction, almost pride, as he walked back towards the huge wooden door.

Placing a hand somewhere that Nick couldn't quite see, the professor unlocked it. The entrance swung open on a hidden hinge and again came that glimpse of somewhere warm and inviting. The smell of old paper and pipe smoke rolled out, and a few peals of laughter that seemed equal parts inviting and cruel.

George was clearly as enthralled by the prospect as Nick, and stood up as if to follow, but the professor's eyes met his, then flicked towards the exhausted figure slumped on the other chair, and shook his head as if to say "not yet."

Then the door was closed and the office was quiet again. George gave Nick a look of disgust as he pushed past, a little too close, and knocked him, sprawling, to the floor. It was some minutes before Nick felt like he had the strength to get back up.

The library was quiet and austere as ever, each bank of bookshelves punctuated by a silent white bust of another long-dead Great Man. Nick sat in a corner, half-slumped over a pile of books, trying to keep his eyes focused on another dry quotation. He liked the library. It was quiet, and perhaps the air wasn't so dry, as his nosebleeds never seemed to happen when he was there. Perhaps he was too afraid to bleed on the books. The fatigue, however, was still very much present, and every stroke of the pen in his notebook was agony.

"Hello!"

The voice behind him was so cheerful as to make his teeth ache. George's face hove into view around the corner.

Nick almost shushed him on reflex, but simply didn't have the energy.

"Hard at it, eh?"

Nick grunted in the affirmative.

"Good good. That's what we like to see. It needs to be your best work this week."

"Why?" Nick just about managed to say.

"Between you and me, I think this might be the week Tom lets us in."

Tom? It took a moment to realise that he was talking about Professor Hughes.

"If we're on top of our game this week, then I'm sure of it. So keep at it, all right?!"

With these words of what he sincerely seemed to think was encouragement, George turned around to leave. As he did so, a thought occurred to Nick.

"George," his voice was barely a whisper.

"Yes?"

"What's my name?"

"Say again?"

"Do you even know my name?"

There wasn't even a pause. No hint of hesitation or embarrassment or awkwardness passed over the face of George Granville before he spoke.

"Listen, I've got to get to a rowing team crew date. You get to work on that essay. This is the week. I can feel it."

"You are not of my house," the priest said, "you are not of my ilk. You have no claim to my bounty. Your trespass shall be the teaching."

It was a nightmare. It was not real. At any moment the shock of awakening would wrench him from this place of onyx and marble.

The knife cut into the base of his neck, sending an electric current of agony through his body. He screamed, and the priest smiled as if hearing a delicate hymn.

Down the knife slid, through skin and fat and muscle. A single smooth motion, long-practised on the part of the skinner. He felt the tip of the blade flick against the bone of his pelvis and even through the pain, the strangeness of that sensation was jarring.

No blood flowed. He should be bleeding. Why was he not bleeding? The skinner had finished another cut and now reached to the new rift in his body. He felt calloused, indifferent fingers push through and into him. They hooked around his flesh and for a moment he felt them against the inside of his skin. Then they began to pull, but it was another five minutes before Nick woke up.

This time he was ready. Struggling through the nightmares and an exhaustion more profound than any he had ever known, Nick had spent all week crafting an essay he was certain was worthy. George's little visit in the library had spurred him on, igniting a burning urge to create something that was so well-argued, so tight and focused, that it would leave his partner's attempt looking like an embarrassment. Nick would pass through the ash wood door, and George would be left behind him. Sometimes he really thought he believed that, while other times Nick knew how absurd it all was, that what he wrote didn't matter to these people. He was so tired, but all he had to do was push through this one tutorial. Just push through and afterwards he would have time to go and see a doctor, to figure out what was wrong with him.

The chair was there, waiting for him, and he steeled himself as he lowered down onto it. It felt more rickety than before, as though the wood was older, and he suspected he might even have gotten a splinter from the fraying frame, but he ignored it. Nick faced Professor Hughes with what he hoped was defiance in his eyes and set his jaw. Beside him, George Granville watched, his expression unreadable. In his hands Nick could see sheets of blank paper. Not even bothering with placeholder text now? He was going to look like a fool.

And yet, there was something else. A strange atmosphere in the room. An odd electricity that Nick couldn't quite describe, but that caused some instinct deep in his brain to urge him: *Run.*

But even if he had wanted to, Nick no longer had the strength.

"I believe you have an essay for us?" came the prompt. Gentle, inviting.

Nick picked up his own printed sheets and tried to choke down the familiar nervousness that threatened to grab his heart as it always did. He nodded, looked down and took a deep breath.

He began to read, his voice shaky and tired, but still just about loud enough to be audible. The words came easier than usual, and there was an odd assurance that he'd never had at any of his previous tutorials. After a few moments he couldn't even hear himself, but it *felt* as though he were speaking with clarity and authority.

As his eyes travelled down the paper, they glided easily over the words, weaving his arguments together. He felt good. Until he reached a word that was gone, obscured by a spreading wave of bright red blood. Another nosebleed? Now? Nick instinctively reached up his upper lip, but it was dry. The stain was still spreading.

Where was it coming from? He shifted his fingers over the bright white paper and realised with a start that it was coming from his hands. There were no cuts or injuries, the blood was simply seeping out, oozing through his skin. Nick looked down at his pale blue shirt to see that it too was now rapidly turning to a deep scarlet.

The professor, George, what were they doing? He looked at them in panic, trying to beg for help, but they simply watched. Professor Hughes looked grimly satisfied, while George looked positively delighted.

Was Nick still speaking? He could feel his lips moving and the words of his essay still seemed to hang in the air, but as though an invisible cord had been passed between them, it was now George who recited them. Nick could barely stay upright now, and could feel the thousands upon thousands of tiny cuts opening on his body, a spreading cascade of minute agonies that he could not endure.

The chair collapsed, dropping him to the floor in a spreading pool of dark blood that stained the worn old carpet of the office. George got to his feet slowly, still reading out the words Nick had written, the research he had done, and knelt down next to him. For the briefest of moments Nick wondered if his partner was going to help him after all, but then George took his clean and spotless sheets of paper and laid them over him, soaking them in crimson.

When they were fully covered, dripping Nick's own blood back onto him, he saw the door at the back standing open. The wood around it was now darkened almost to black, and shone with a brilliant lustre. Beyond the threshold lay George's future: a long, unbroken tradition of learning and authority.

As he walked past Nick, bleeding out on the floor, George stopped.

"Thanks for this," he said, politely. "Couldn't have done it without you."

There was the briefest of pauses, as though he were trying to recall Nick's name, then he and the professor walked through the ash wood door and closed it behind them.

The Lovers

Lynda E Rucker

The book was wedged into the shelf in a way that made Kristen think someone had tried to hide it. Concealing it would hardly have been difficult; it was one of *those* bookstores, jammed from floor to ceiling, volumes double- and triple-stacked, some faded with age, some bent. Dust, and the smell of mould, was everywhere. She'd never been in the shop before, which was tucked away on a side street, but she knew its type, the kind of place where you felt as though you weren't buying the books so much as you were liberating them.

The volume had been shoved not just atop one of those triple-stacked rows but wedged into the overhang from the shelf above. Kristen felt its cover graze her knuckles as she was reaching for a different book balanced on the top of the row. She had to pry it loose to free it.

Her first instinct was to put it right back. It was a hardcover book with a sickly yellow cover that had nothing printed on it at all. The pages were rough cut, uneven to the touch as she ran her finger down the fore edge. She opened it; inside, it was as blank as the cover. Some kind of journal, but no one had ever written in it.

She did not remember adding it to the top of her little stack of half a dozen other books, but later, as she was waiting in the pub for Greta, she opened her bag to review her treasures and there it was – jammed in between an old orange spine Penguin of Graham Greene's *The End of the Affair* and a terrific U.S. edition of Shirley Jackson's *The Haunting of Hill House*, an old Fawcett paperback that conceptualized Eleanor as a Gothic heroine with flowing hair and a single candle on a darkened staircase – like an unwelcome prize the shop owner had slipped in when she wasn't looking.

"Sorry I'm late!"

Greta swept into the seat across from her like the whirlwind she was, plonked a to-go cup of coffee on the table and promptly knocked it over.

Kristen yelped and grabbed her books, raising them to safety as a river of coffee cascaded into her lap.

"Oh shit. Oh shit, I'm sorry." Greta pulled a pack of tissues out of her bag and thrust an ineffectual wad across the table at her.

"It's fine," Kristen said; the coffee had been lukewarm and was soaking clammily into her jeans. A waitress appeared with a cloth and mopped up what was on the table, and somewhere in the flurry of activity Greta set a gin and tonic in front of her, so that was all right.

"Jesus," Greta said. "I'm sorry, I'm all out of sorts, you won't believe who rang me a little while ago—"

Kristen said, "I think I accidentally bought a haunted book—"

They both stopped, laughed, and simultaneously gestured at the other. "You first."

"No, you," Kristen said, and since she had the last word Greta got the next one.

"Fucking Paul, that's who," Greta said. "The fucking nerve." She drew her mouth down, making a face as she spoke in a low, doltish voice. "I miss you. I was wrong. Blah blah blah."

"What did you *say?*"

An expression flickered across Greta's face that Kristen couldn't read. "I—I said I'd meet him."

"*Greta!*"

She put a hand up. Stop sign. "I know. *I know.* I was gonna lie to you, you know, say I gave him a piece of my mind, but, well. Don't look at me like that!"

"When and where? I'm going with you."

"Tomorrow, and you so are not."

"What time? I'm going to ring you. Twenty minutes after you meet him. And remind you of all the shitty things he's done to you over the past year—"

"You're not going to do any of those things," Greta said in her case-closed voice. "Now, what's this about a haunted book?"

Kristen passed her the volume with the sickly yellow cover. "This weird thing," she said. "It's just a blank journal, somebody must've left it in the bookstore by accident and they just shelved it because they've no idea what they have in there. I picked it up and put it down only I must not have because here it is."

"Ooh," Greta said. "Like a cursed thing in a horror movie you can't get rid of. I bet if you put it in the bin, it would be on your pillow when you got home."

"Don't."

"It isn't blank," Greta went on. She held it up. On the very first page, opposite the inside cover, a careful calligraphic hand had written "The Lovers."

"That's weird. I must not have looked inside the cover."

"Sounds racy." Greta flipped through the rest of the pages with a disappointed look on her face. "Or not. Oh, here's something. 'Journeys end in lovers meeting.'"

"Huh. Shakespeare. *Or*. If you want to be creepy about it." Kristen picked up the copy of *Hill House* and waved it at her. "When your lover is an actual demonic house."

Greta was her usual impervious self. "That's as far as the ostensible author got, hm? A title and a little light plagiarism. I hope you didn't pay too much for it, you're right about the rest of it being blank."

"I don't think I paid anything for it at all," Kristen said, but rummaging back through the plastic bag the shop owner had given her, she couldn't find a receipt. "Anyway. Paul. What the hell, Greta?"

"Would you believe me if I said I was going to let him debase himself, apologize profusely and beg me to come back and *then* tell him to fuck off?"

"No."

"Well." Greta sighed. "You'd be right."

Kristen took a sip of her drink and said it: "*Men*."

"Fucking *men*."

They drank until the pub closed. Kristen hadn't meant to. She had work in the morning, and it was a long trip home by tube and bus to her sister's place in Uxbridge. Polly had grudgingly rented her the guest room in the bungalow she shared with her dull husband and two squabbling children after a houseshare in Shoreditch had fallen through.

Losing your home wasn't the actual worst thing about breaking up with someone, but it was certainly one of many indignities that accompanied it.

Polly seemed determined to price the room at a rate that ensured Kristen wouldn't be in any hurry to stick around, as though the actual living conditions themselves were so desirable that no one in their right mind would move on otherwise. Really it was a surprise that Polly was as eager as she was for this to be a short-term thing, given all the opportunities it presented for her to play up the role of the sane, responsible older sister.

It wasn't that Polly tried to pretend she was in love with her husband and that her children were a source of delight; on the contrary, she loved to moan about how miserable it made her, but the fact that she endured it all was, she clearly felt, a marker of maturity. "It never occurs to her that she's not exactly *selling* it as a lifestyle," Kristen said to Greta as the evening wore on and the alcohol made everything either funny or sad. They collapsed into giggles. It wasn't *that* funny, though, Kristen thought as the bus lumbered to a stop and she got off and trudged up toward Polly's place. Polly had actually been fun, once, when they were kids, even into their early twenties – more so than Kristen. Polly had always been the one up for the next party, effortlessly chic, with a string of more-or-less boyfriends and just enough of a cocaine habit to be fashionable. Kristen, by comparison, had been the dowdy, bookish sister. When Polly hastily married John, Kristen had been aghast – he was the kind of man they'd have laughed at a year before the wedding, a pompous, boring windbag, and unattractive to boot. But Polly had appeared suddenly eager to embark on a new life as a suburban mum, so suddenly you'd have thought she was bewitched, but it was a decade now and counting.

After she'd moved in with them, Kristen had been determined to see something more in him – after all, Polly had married him, and Kristen felt she herself was often too quick to judge – but the fact of the matter was, there really was nothing there. If she'd read John in story, she'd have thought him lazily sketched, but he was just that, a living caricature of a certain type of man who had been boring both women and other men since time out of mind. There had probably been a prehistoric version of John, she thought: one who obsessively collected something like spearheads or whatever and droned on to anyone who would listen about the migratory habits of some species or other, one that wasn't even any good for food, so the information was useless as well as dull.

The mental image of John as a boring hunter-gatherer actually cheered her up a bit so that when she stepped though the front door she must have been smiling a little. "Well, *you* look like the cat that's swallowed the canary," Polly said from her seat on the living room sofa.

Kristen jumped. "You're up late."

"Not as late as you," Polly said, which probably made some kind of sense in her head.

Kristen swallowed a retort.

"It's not setting a good example for Anna and Noah," Polly went on, and with that Kristen thought she was joking, because she had to be, and yet she just barrelled right on. "When John and I invited you into our home, we didn't think it would be like this."

Like what, Kristen started to say, but Polly wasn't waiting.

"Out at all hours— *Are you laughing at me?*"

Kristen couldn't help it. This was *Polly*, of all people!

"Look, if it's so funny to you, then I'll just move straight to the point. We need you out of here. Sooner rather than later. It's a huge strain on all of us."

Kristen, leaning on the door frame, feeling every single one of the – five? six? more – drinks she'd had, tried to pull herself together and look serious. "You're absolutely right, Pol. I've been thinking the very same thing. I'll be out by the end of the month."

"Good," Polly said, looking as though she'd been robbed of the row she'd geared herself up for. "Fine. It's settled, then."

"Good," Kristen said back at her, but in her room it hit her. She suddenly felt sober. *Why did I say that? Fuck. Fuck.* There just wasn't anywhere to rent, it was as simple as that, unless she wanted to move into some ghastly ten-person house with a bunch of feckless twenty-somethings. You had to be a banker or something to afford anything decent in London, and buying was entirely out of the question. She could probably crash on a sofa at Greta's or with another friend for a week or two, but no one had any space for her long term.

She'd been nodding off on the way home, but now she was stressed and wide awake. She had to leave for work in a few hours. She reached for the books she'd bought – not that she'd have anywhere to put them now – and when she upended the bag, the journal slid out on top again.

She realized then what the colour reminded her of. Not a colour she'd ever seen in real life, only in her imagination. It was the colour from the story "The Yellow Wallpaper". She pulled a volume off one of her shelves and thumbed through it until she found the line: "repellent, almost revolting: a smouldering, unclean yellow." And the narrator's husband, another boring John – although it was impossible to imagine Pol in the narrator's position, driven to a nervous breakdown. Pol driving everyone else *to* a breakdown, more like.

Kristen opened the journal again. How had she missed that homemade title page? "The Lovers," and then on the next page that line – *journeys end in lovers meeting* – poignancy poisoned by the Jackson rendering.

She wondered if she should return the book to the shop. If someone had lost it, they might want it back. Then again, there was no telling how long it had been there. Forever, judging by the look of it.

She turned a few more pages and there was writing there, after all, in that same careful hand. Kristen began to read. It was the saddest story she had ever encountered. She found herself wishing she had never picked up the book and yet she couldn't stop, even as the tears streamed down her face.

The next day at work was horrible. It was never great – Kristen's job at a big multinational company that, like most multinational companies, did varied and vaguely sinister things, involved inputting information into spreadsheets and databases and was so intensely boring that she couldn't bear to talk about it – but this day was especially bad, and not just because it seemed like her alarm went off about five minutes after she drifted off and dreamed she was reading something unspeakably tragic. It must have been a dream, and anyway, she had other things to worry about, specifically where she was going to live. She'd put some of her stuff into storage when she moved into Polly's; could you live in a storage unit? Or maybe she should just chuck it all and go travelling, but you needed money to do that and last she'd checked she had £300 in her account; plus you couldn't just go over to Europe and pick up a job anymore, could you? Maybe she should move up north where everyone said you could still afford things, but she didn't know anyone there. Jesus. She felt that somewhere along the way she had fucked her life up, badly, but she couldn't work out where the error had been. Breaking up with Andy? Moving in with him in the first place? Not studying something sensible at university so she could get a job that paid her a lot of money?

At the end of the work day she was exhausted, but the thought of going back to Polly's house made her feel even more exhausted. No point in ringing Greta, who was no doubt doing something ill-advised with Paul. She scrolled through her phone contacts. It felt like her fingers had a mind of their own when they selected one and punched the phone icon.

"Hey," she said when Nick answered. "Want to get a drink?"

He looked great when he sauntered into the French House in Soho, pushing past the crowds and making his way to the table in the back she'd claimed for them.

"This is a surprise," he said, even though it surely wasn't.

She'd downed two quick espressos before heading over and still felt like she was sleepwalking. "I just thought," she said, and she had no idea how to complete the sentence. What *had* she just thought?

They said honesty was the best policy. "My life's gone to shit," she said, "how's yours?"

He laughed. That easy laugh. It was – no, it wasn't the most attractive thing about him, but only because *everything* was the most attractive thing about him. "You first," he said, and then, "no, I'll get you a drink first."

She should say a Coke so she said a whiskey, and make it a double – he laughed again, and when he came back, the mere half pint he'd bought himself felt like a rebuke. "So, my sister's kicking me out," she said. "In two weeks."

"Obviously," he said, "if you ever need a place…"

"Thanks," she said. They both knew she wouldn't take him up on it but they also both knew he had to make the offer.

She knocked the whiskey back with a few quick gulps.

"Hey," he said. "I actually got you something good there."

"Sorry," she said, and wiped her mouth with the back of her hand. "I'll get the next round."

He gestured at his drink. "I'm good for the moment."

"Right." She got herself another whiskey and sat back down. "I'm sorry," she said. "This is a shitty thing to do, invite you here to moan about where my life's gone wrong. Tell me what you've been up to."

She lowered her voice as she spoke because she could see from the corner of her eye that there was a couple at the next table leaning over a bit, as though they were eavesdropping.

Nick didn't seem to notice them. He was working on a new project, an installation – she should come, he'd send her an invite – and he'd been hired to create some paintings for a film, and things were good, really, good enough that he'd cut his teaching hours. "And how about you?" he said. "Still writing?"

It felt like he was throwing her a bone. She'd wanted to be a writer. That was why she had the excruciating job, the one that was too dull to talk or think about, because she was going to make it big and she wouldn't need a job any longer (did that even happen to writers any more?) only the problem was that to be a writer, you had to do more than love storytelling, and books, and reading, and you had to do more than just want it more than you wanted anything

You had to actually write things. And not just shit in your journal.

"Working on something!" she said, and as she said it, she saw in his face that he knew she was lying, so she kept going. "It's pretty weird," she went on. "It's called 'The Lovers'. It's about how it's basically doomed between men and women, how you can never meet at the right juncture – like the passion isn't there, so you can bear one another but you're also dying of boredom, or the passion is there so you end up tearing one another to bits, destroying one another really—" She wanted to stop talking. She was going to say too much, give herself away. "I don't know," she said. "I'm still in the middle of working it all out, I don't want to talk about it too much."

"Well, when you figure it out, shoot it over my way. I'd love to read it."

Those people at the next table listening weren't even trying to hide it now. She turned to say something withering to them, but there was no one there.

"You want to get out of here? Go back to your place?"

He looked at his half pint. He'd barely touched it. Was he seriously debating whether he'd rather have the rest of what was in his glass or her?

Embarrassed, she tried to backtrack, said, "Did you see those people?" but then he was pushing his chair back. "Let's go."

"They were listening to us," she said, but he didn't hear her, or didn't answer.

Later, lying in bed, she started to tell him a little bit about the journal. She didn't know why she brought it up. "I had a dream about it," she said. "That I was reading it, and the story was so heartbreaking I couldn't stop crying, but I couldn't remember any of it when I woke up."

While she talked, Nick said, "Mmm" and stroked her thigh. He wasn't really the kind of person you talked to about things like haunted books and dreams.

After he fell asleep she lay next to him and wondered whether she could try to make some kind of relationship out of whatever this was, just so she could have somewhere to land while she figured out what she was going to do next. But that was crazy. She might as well go back to Andy if she was willing to put up with anything for the sake of a roof over her head. Kristen quietly got dressed and left, only realizing once she was out on the just street how late it was. On the one hand, she risked facing another disapproving lecture from Polly when she got home. On the other hand, surely Polly had that out of her system now that she was leaving. And on the third hand, she needed a change of clothes so she could go to work the next morning so she had to leave anyway. She sure wasn't going to turn up the next day with walk-of-shame written all over her.

It was late, and the street Nick lived on was empty. Above, thick clouds scudded in front of a full moon. There were footfalls in the street, and she turned but saw no one. Up ahead, she could see the bus approaching the stop near the corner and she ran to catch it.

She once again had the sensation that there were two people nearby, this time in the seat behind her, but the bus was nearly empty. All the same, she sat sideways with her back to the window until the bus dropped her off at a tube station.

It took well over an hour to get back to Polly's, and this time, fortunately, no one was awake. She got the book out from where she'd hidden it that morning before she left for work. She didn't know why she'd had the urge to hide it; even if she suspected anyone in the house was the snooping type, everyone would be away at school or work, plus it didn't *matter* if anyone saw it. But it did. She wanted it only for herself.

And yet she couldn't help noticing something she hadn't before: it had an unwholesome smell about it to accompany its unpleasant colour. The yellow was in fact more vile than she had realized in the shop or the pub – staring at it now in her room with the light on, it made her think of the kind of things that oozed out of you when you were sick. Pus. Vomit.

She looked at her hands. Were her fingertips stained the lightest, most hideous yellow? No, of course they weren't. It was her imagination.

She was so tired, but she opened it and began to read where she'd left off the previous night. This installment was even more heartbreaking than the last one. Later, she dreamed: about being followed, about getting lost, and of figures without faces that copulated repetitively, endlessly, without joy or purpose.

When her alarm went off the next morning, she was still sprawled on top of the duvet in her clothes.

She woke up to a text from Nick: *Where'd you go?* And one from Greta not long after: *Fucking Paul.* She didn't answer either of them. An even worse day at work followed. She was jittery, and made several errors. She had a pounding headache.

In the afternoon, Greta again: *Drink?*

Kristen typed back: *Fuck yeah.*

Five p.m. couldn't come quickly enough. Some of her coworkers were going out for a drink as well but she dodged them and made her way back to the pub where she and Greta had met the other day. She went by the bookstore first – half-expecting it to not be there – but it was, of course, although it had a sign on the window: *Closed, family emergency.*

Family emergency. Kristen thought about the phrase as she sat waiting for Greta. You ought to be able to use a similar phrase to opt out in any number of circumstances. Heartbreak emergency. Housing emergency. At least a family emergency implied that you *had* a family, people around you who actually gave a shit whether you lived or died.

And here was Greta, already with drinks for both of them.

"Fucking Paul, you won't believe—"

"I'm thinking of getting back together with Andy—"

They both stopped, again, but this time it was Greta who waved Kristen on. "Forget Paul, it's a stupid story and you actually will believe it to the point of 'I told you so'. What the fuck is this *getting back together with Andy* bullshit?"

Kristen hadn't even been thinking it until she said it. "I don't know. Things are weird. And I have to move out of Pol's."

"Aw, babe. You can stay at my place. You know that being with a guy so that you have a place to live makes you, like, basically a prostitute, right? I know housing is tight but come on."

Kristen rolled her eyes. "Stop it, Greta, it's not just *a guy*, it's Andy."

"Who did the following things." Greta held up her hand and pushed down one beringed finger for every fault she enumerated. "Completely did not listen to you *ever*, belittled your ambition, called you selfish and immature and let's not forget, knocked you down in the course of an argument."

"It was a shove. He didn't mean to."

"What? What is this about, Kristen? You're over him, it's been months."

But she wasn't. She never would be. They had been together for five years, after all. You didn't just brush that away. She'd had to make herself so hard to do it, to leave him. He had cried and asked her not to. She could go back. As easy as that. Five months were nothing.

"It's the book," she said.

"What book?"

"The one, you know, I had here the other night." Greta was looking at her expectantly, and she began stumbling over her words, knowing how she must sound. "I took it home and…there was a story in there after all."

"What do you mean?"

"There were words written in it. It was so sad."

"There wasn't anything in it. Just the title and that weird quote. We looked all the way through it, sitting right here at this table. Remember that time when you were sleepwalking? Is this like that?"

"And I keep thinking." She could feel tears welling up as she spoke and she willed them to go away. "I keep thinking people are following me. It's like there is always this presence just out of my vision or hearing, but they're there. Two of them."

Greta's expression had become concerned. Kristen could see that she was trying to think what to say, and that of course she was out of her depth. She instantly felt ashamed.

"I mean, not *really* following me. I know it's my imagination. Not like those people," and she half-turned, but there was no one at the table she meant although she'd been sure of it. "I… guess they left."

"Kristen. There hasn't been anyone there."

She took a sip of her drink. "Let's talk about you."

"Let's *not*. Look, do you have anyone to…talk to?"

"What, as in 'you need to see a doctor, Kristen'? Just forget it, okay?"

"That's not the kind of thing you just forget."

"Oooh." Kristen waved her hands. "My friend read a book and thought some people were nearby but there weren't. Better section her."

"I didn't say that."

"After all, she's been locked up before. And hey, at least she'd have a place to stay."

"Kris. Stop."

"It's what you're thinking, isn't it?"

"I'm not thinking anything."

"I'm going," Kristen said, not without downing the rest of her drink first, and Greta tried to grab her arm as she stood up but she bolted for the door and shoved it open and ran down the street as hard as she could. It felt good to run like that, with abandon like she was a kid, and she kept it up until her lungs were burning and she had to stop and bend over to catch her breath.

It was amazing how everybody saw you the same way in the end, even someone like Greta who was supposed to be your best friend. No matter what, when it came down to it, you were just the crazy girl. Probably Pol had said something similar to John. Made it sound like there was something wrong with her, like she was *dangerous* and that was why they wanted her to leave.

She didn't want to go back there. For a while she just walked, but then her legs started to ache. She stopped in at the next pub she came to that wasn't heaving, got a drink and found herself a table in a corner. She took out her phone; Greta had been ringing and texting her. She turned it off.

In her bag she had the journal. She couldn't remember whether or not she'd deliberately taken it with her when she left for work in the morning but it didn't matter, it was here now, and she opened it to pick up where she'd left off. But it wasn't the same. There had been an element of melancholy beauty to the story before, but that seemed like it was gone now. It was the yellow, she thought, that sickly yellow colour had infected it, and it was spreading its spores now, turning the story she read bilious and rotten. When she looked up from the page, it had infected her as well; a kind of yellow film across everything and everyone as she saw them for what they really were, lonely and desperate.

Kristen closed her eyes, like that could reset it, but the yellow was there in the dark behind her eyelids as well. She opened them again and thought *I could just leave it here, I could just get up and go* but wouldn't that be irresponsible, mightn't someone else find it, and anyway, she really didn't want to.

The air was close and suffocating. Outside, it had started to rain, and when she pushed open the door, she felt them just at her left elbow. She knew if she turned her head to look directly at them they would vanish.

They fell into step with her as she made her way down the rain-spattered pavement. She wanted to talk to them. She wanted to tell them how important their story was, how the world should know their story because it was a story everyone could tell, the story of that unspeakable loss and betrayal. How it was to know with every cell in your body that if you were lost at the end of the world that the other person would find you, and how it was to find yourself there and slowly realize that they would never come for you after all.

As they continued to walk together, the three of them, they began to press in on her uncomfortably. She didn't like that. She appreciated the way they had always kept their distance. She need only turn and look at them, though, and they would go, but if she did that, she would be alone again.

They walked on. They walked across Soho and on into Islington, where she and Andy had lived – was it a deliberate cruelty that they led her there? And they began to speak to her, as though they no longer needed the journal as a conduit. Their voices were like she imagined the voices of snakes might sound, hissing their stories at her, each of them telling it differently, implicitly calling the other a liar. And like snakes, they were there at the creation, the origin story that brought it all down in the first place: sin and temptation, knowledge and fleshly delights. Now she really wanted them to leave her, and she walked faster, they were through the other side of Islington now and into Dalston, and she turned to look at each of them, but they weren't hiding themselves any longer.

They were emaciated, naked figures, and where their faces should have been they had only enormous, devouring mouths, yet despite their gauntness, their genitals were exaggerated, like statues she'd seen of ancient fertility figures, an erect phallus on one and on the other an absurdly prominent vulva: impossible anatomy, and when walking faster and staring at them didn't deter them she stopped in the middle of the pavement and shouted. She screamed for them to stop and to leave her alone, but all that happened was that they drew closer to her still, clung to her, while pedestrians parted ways around her, pointedly ignoring her, giving them all a wide berth.

She was growing weary, and she had the feeling that they could continue forever. They were in Stoke Newington now, past the police station – would she go in? could they help? – and onwards, this was familiar territory, she and Polly had shared a flat here briefly about 15 years and a lifetime ago.

At the entrance to Abney Park Cemetery she stopped. She had come here more days than not during those few months when she and Polly lived nearby, before everything went wrong and they'd locked her up. The cemetery would be closing soon but it didn't matter now. She rummaged in her bag for the journal, but she must have lost it somewhere along the way.

"I don't have it any longer," she said to them.

The rain had passed, but night was drawing in, a chill forming on the air and the path where she stood just inside the entrance.

"I can't help you," she said to them, and headed up one of the lanes toward broken headstones long since claimed by ivy.

Yet they would not be dissuaded. They no longer flanked her, but they didn't need to. They had the measure of her now.

Journeys end in lovers meeting.

She found what she was searching for, a small grove of ash trees; weren't they said to be somehow sacred? She supposed there were people who might go to a church, in a similar circumstance, but if anyone could help her, it was the older gods. Surely if she could unleash whatever she had from the pages of that foul book, she could also draw out this ancient, protective energy.

But she saw them from the grove, and they were coming her way, pale figures stark in the gathering twilight. What kind of prayers did old gods want? She sank to the earth, plunged her fingers deep into the loamy dirt.

They reminded her of spiders now, all spindly legs and arms that reached for her. And those hollow, monstrous mouths, open wide and getting closer.

They were so lost, and so sorrowful, and so very hungry.

Temperance

Gary Budden

Blown plaster hit the floor; it crunched like dry bone beneath my work boots. Horsehair floated in the dust. The building's brickwork was now visible beneath an ancient skim coat the colour of smokers' teeth. Victorian, Edwardian maybe. From whenever they still added animal hair to the render; to strengthen it, so I'd been told. Old enough. It would all need replastering, and that would mean getting in those dickheads Danny and Ted from Ponders End; unless I found someone else to do the job, of course. But time was against me, I lacked the energy to find anyone else, and I couldn't do it myself.

Paying rent and a mortgage simultaneously was killing me, as was the time taken off paid work to stand here inhaling plaster dust and chipping away until, somehow, a home was formed. Elizabeth's emotional distress at the amount of time the project was taking was weighing on my chest like pig iron. Everything needed doing, and it needed to be done faster. In every sense, I was failing.

Cheerful texts from friends and colleagues asking, 'So when's the house party?' spun me into a blind rage. I replied, 'Can't wait to have you over soon!', with a smiley face at the end of the message, even as I fantasised taking the sledgehammer on loan from Elizabeth's father to the building's foundations, toppling the place into the road, killing all inside and any passing pedestrians, damaging the vehicles of my neighbours, causing a scene worthy of the local news.

The exposed brickwork was a patchwork of terracotta and orange-reds, speckles of yellowy-white and charcoal blackness. It brought to mind my grandmother, her old and failing skin in the weeks before she passed away, lying mute but aware in a hospital bed in Canterbury as gentle drizzle fell outside. We had loved each other dearly, though I rarely mentioned this to people. It didn't seem fitting; too cloying and sentimental, almost absurd.

I was surprised to find that I dreamt of her for months after her death, vivid and too-real, as she calmly asked me what I was doing with my life. I had always assumed these visitations were a thing of fiction, tropes in sentimental American films, or the stuff of old folklore. So, it felt like a cliché, but there she was. She was younger when she visited me, at an age I had never known her, a respectable and well-turned-out secretarial woman from 1950s north London. In the dreams, I tried to answer her calm questioning but found my vocal cords were frozen. The words were there, inside me, but they would not come no matter how hard I tried.

I wished she could see me in this room – doing something, finally, with my life. Chipping away. Moving forward, one chisel blow and piece of blown plaster at a time. Bricks and cement, a twenty-five-year debt, a real commitment to something, an outdoor space I didn't have to share with anyone but my fiancée. These were the modest dreams I was near to achieving.

I swung my lump hammer lazily onto another piece of loose plaster and it fell into the rubble with a thump. A dust cloud rose. Strands of scratchy horsehair hovered like quivering damselflies.

I was breathing heavily through a mask that covered my mouth and nose. Theoretically, it was filtering the particles and muck that hung miasmic in the air. I was a large man, and the cheap mask's straps cut tightly and painfully into the back of my head. It was too small for me, and I hadn't bothered to try to find any with a better fit. I often struggled to find gear that fit me comfortably, and I had realised long ago that no one cared much for any complaints. Elizabeth thought it cute, endearing, and that I should laugh such things off.

Despite my mask, I coughed roughly like an asthmatic. Too many cigarettes out in the garden; the lines of cocaine; the pollution and exhaust fumes of the A10 as we drove open-windowed to B&Q and Selco and to the McDonalds drive-through; inhalation of particles of cement, plaster, brick, fibreglass insulation, horsehair, sawdust, and other unnamed substances. The soft lagging we spent days pushing and stapling into the newly constructed stud walls, I read on online forums, would lacerate the lungs if inhaled in any great quantity. It was a price I would gladly pay for security and ascending the social ladder; and I had my mask.

I thought of all the damage I'd done to myself over the years and wondered if any more would make a difference. The bottomless pouches of tobacco, the nights that always became mornings, the rooms of dust and smoke and endless white lines stretching off into the darkness.

As the blown plaster settled, I felt grit in my vision, an eyeball I wanted to scratch and rub if that didn't mean transferring more dirt to my eyes. My mask was soaked with sweat, thirsty dust clinging to the moisture.

There was always the dust.

That was when I saw the figure.

It, her, him, them, all and none would be fitting.

I was coughing my lungs up, my eyes gritty and wet, the straps of a cheap face mask cutting into the back of my skull when I saw the towering being, perhaps eight feet tall, standing in the swirling plumes of dust and horsehair that filled the gutted living room of this flat on this suburban street in this backwater of outer north London. My eyes were streaming, agitated and aggravated by the dust. To an outside observer it would look like I was crying in rapture.

The figure leisurely spread a pair of giant wings, feathered like those of the grey herons I often saw standing motionless by the north London canals and the New River, and turned its face to look directly at me. The expression it wore expressed an emotion I had never encountered in my life to this date; a feeling unknown to me, perhaps to all but the furthest fringes of humankind. My mind scrambled to find words that could approximate a description of what I was seeing: Beatific. Seraphic. Terrible. Awesome. But, somehow urgent and imploring. How can I describe its face? Something I would never be able to forget, despite my attempts to drown it in the bottle. I feel that its eyes are still looking into me, yet I am unable to picture it or pin it down any time I attempt to draw or describe it. The image escapes me like a shadow chased away by the sun.

Dust fell like golden confetti from a place impossibly high above.

The figure's skin had a bluish tint and was textured like marble, or so it looked. I wanted to touch it, feel it's coolness, discover if the skin was pliant as mortal flesh or hard as stone. But I knew this was inappropriate, unacceptable. The being wore the simple and flowing robes of a peasant in an equatorial region. It was beautiful.

Its lips moved gently, as if it were trying to soothe a frightened child, yet the voice that emerged filled the entire room, with a bass frequency that I felt rising up through the floor into my feet and legs; like the sound-systems from the parties back in the day, filling my entire being. More blown plaster crashed to the floor, and as my being trembled and vibrated, I thought of my grandmother again. Her mischievous smile; her watercolour painting of a lonely skiff on a Welsh lake, framed by dark mountains; the way she looked at me with tearful recognition the evening before she died.

I started to cry.

I couldn't understand the language being spoken. I was English, from the southeast, monolingual, with a moderate gift for words that I'd never really used other than to wind people up in pubs or prove an obscure point. I had always felt bad about this, but had done nothing to change it. When would I find the time? I had work to do.

Inscrutable words that felt like tectonic shift filled the inside of my skull with a painful pressure. My temples throbbed; my teeth ached. I pictured them bursting in sharp clouds of blood, enamel, and yellow plaque. I felt like I was on the verge of overdosing, my heart pounding furiously, acrid sweat bathing me, a tidal wave of rising anxiety. Too much. I couldn't handle it. Stop. Stop. Please.

But what was being said seemed of crucial importance if only I could grasp the meaning. The world was there for me to understand, for all of us to interpret and gain meaning from, if only we could speak its language. The cruellest of jokes: to know there was so much I would never know. That none of us would. Why couldn't I understand? Here I was being given an opportunity, and I was wasting it, as always.

I saw a vision of myself on my grandmother's skiff, sailing towards the dark mountains.

The muscular heron wings flapped slowly in the dust as she continued to speak. We made eye contact.

My god of emptiness, EN1.

The Enfield angel.

My devil in the dust.

The heron. The egret. My regret.

Each word rattled my being and made my blood pulse. I felt the stirring of an erection as I continued to weep until the sobs morphed and I began to laugh deeply, dangerously and recklessly, the sound muffled inside my mask, as tears dripped down my face. I considered that this was what losing it felt like.

Could the neighbours upstairs hear what was happening?

The Enfield angel watched me silently as I laughed.

Whatever message was being imparted to me was now finished. The being smiled kindly and disappeared with a beating of its heron wings in the shimmer of falling brick and plaster dust that continued to fall, sticking to the sweat on my arms and neck.

Bereft at its disappearance, I rubbed my eyes, regretting it instantly as I felt the dust and grit scour my vision.

I coughed like an old, dying man, my chest racking and heaving, blinking in pain. I spat on the floor. My mind swam with images of heron wings and marble skin, of my grandmother smiling, of a desert of plaster and brick dust, dunes stretching off interminably into the horizon.

I tried to rationalise what had happened. I was strung out on speedy own-brand instant coffee that I swore was corroding my stomach lining, and from the line of coke I'd snorted earlier off the back of my iPhone. I was jittery with borrowed energy, racking up an ever-increasing debt. The greasy breakfast bap I'd grabbed quickly from the McDonalds drive-through was now repeating on me; plastic egg and processed sausage. I'd been awake since five thirty that morning, as I had been for the previous seven days straight. At the flat by seven. Crack on, get the work done. That was the mantra. The project had to be finished; no matter how far out of my depth I had swum, I clung to a belief that the opposite shoreline would soon become visible. I kept going. I'll admit I had something to prove, that I wouldn't flake out or give up or throw in the towel. I wanted Elizabeth to see that I could do it. To show her old man I wasn't useless, that I could go the distance.

I often complained that people in contemporary society wanted everything immediately, instant gratification, throwing their toys out of the pram if they didn't get it. Outraged if an Amazon delivery was a day late, tutting if the queue at Costa was too long. I was prey to this disease myself, and hated myself for it.

Before-and-after renovation photos cut out something crucial – the middle. The relentless, grinding slog.

But life owed me nothing. Anything good within the world had to be worked for. I couldn't just jack it all in – was this what the Enfield angel had been trying to tell me?

I envied it its muscular heron wings, its ability to escape all of this.

When I saw Elizabeth furiously scanning the Instagram accounts of other doer-uppers – doe-eyed blonde girls out in Surrey named Imogen or Harriet or Chloe; clean, respectable blank-faced men with pattern baldness standing beside them, standing in front of their new brickslip walls – I wanted to swat her phone out of her hand, stamp on it and crush it to pieces. The only reality was sweat and dust and toil. Always the dust. The Christians say 'All are of the dust, and all turn to dust again', and maybe they are correct. When chipping away at the remains of old London houses, destined to have their interiors torn down and rebuilt for generations, it was hard to argue with.

My heart was still pounding, but calming down. I was lonely, tired, and ill, and I'd always had a vivid imagination. My head up in the clouds, my nan always said. Elizabeth too. A head stuck in books or obsessively tracking the discographies of pioneering British hardcore acts was somehow worse than a face glued to a mobile phone screen.

I needed to sleep. People see funny things when they're strung out and wired, I told myself, though it had never happened to me before. That's what it was, a trick of the light and the dust and a brain misfiring. But did those things *really* happen, or had I learned it from fiction? I'd barely hallucinated on mushrooms and acid. But perhaps caffeine and tiredness could do this.

I told myself I'd take a day off tomorrow. Catch up on some shuteye, a day's detox. Some decent food, plenty of water.

But I knew what I'd seen. The heron-winged angel of EN1 had really been there even if it was just my misfiring synapses creating their own reality. My imagination was part of reality, was it not? I tried to bat away the thought as the implications were too much right now.

I walked back into the kitchen, removing my mask, and washing my face with water from the cold tap. It felt beautiful, sharply cold and refreshing.

I boiled the kettle and made an instant black coffee with a spoonful of white sugar. I chopped out another line of coke to get me through the morning's work, balancing my iPhone on some boxes of kitchen gear awaiting unpacking. The others would be here soon, and I didn't want to do this around them. I didn't want to share either. They couldn't know I was far more like them than they thought.

I stepped out into the garden with my coffee, happy again and my face tingling. My mouth was dust-dry. It was still cool outside, but a haze in the air promised the deep warmth of the September heatwave we were living though. The heat of the last few days had felt animal, sweaty and alive, like the body of an ancient predator pressed close against me.

Immediately, I gagged and sputtered. Strands of spider silk from the web I had just accidentally destroyed caught in my mouth, snagged in my stubble and hair. I spasmed involuntarily as I saw a frantic orb weaver spider spinning in mid-air on an invisible and dislocated section of web. It was fat and juicy, the width of a two-pound coin, golden and charcoal black. I shuddered, feeling thousands of its kind crawling rapidly over my skin.

The spider landed gracefully on the floor, and I looked at it for a second. It was beautiful, and I killed it. Smeared it across the concrete with my boot. I wasn't in the mood for this bullshit.

I rolled a cigarette from my pouch, spitting stray flakes of tobacco that had stuck to my lip. I had theoretically quit a year ago, and told Elizabeth I was now just having a few fags with the workmen, with my cousin who was doing the kitchen, with the plasterers, a bonding thing, you know? It was a stressful time. I needed to be one of the guys. She didn't believe me, but I maintained the lie regardless. The stress, I reassured myself, had led me back to Tesco's cigarette counter, waiting impatiently in line behind locals buying lottery tickets.

Whenever I tried to examine them, my weaknesses and vices and addictions scurried out of the light like a nest of disturbed arachnids. There'd be time for all that when the renovation was complete. Time to settle, to think, to give things up.

The uneven concrete that led up to the overgrown garden was punctuated with weeds. Fizzing with caffeine, cocaine, and nicotine, I took in the webs of orb weavers strung across the garden and beaded with dew soon to burn off in the coming heat. I counted ten at least of them, these creatures relentlessly spinning webs that looked like star charts or maps of the universe.

Every morning I grabbed a broom and destroyed their morbid constellations. But today I thought I'd let the webs be.

I wandered into the garden, dodging the webs, and took a deep breath of morning air. Movement in the grass tickled my peripheral vision.

I bent down to see a stag beetle on its back, legs whirring like a mechanical toy. Most of its thorax had been eaten away and inside was a mass of ants moving like boiling water, devouring the beetle from the inside. I filmed this on my phone and sent it to a few friends.

I returned to the backdoor step and sat down, smoking and trembling at the lingering feeling of the Enfield angel's words. I buzzed with stimulants. My erection had now subsided.

Overhead, something massive and slow flew over the garden, heavy wings beating like the pulsing of a heart.

A grey heron, on its way to the New River.

I was staying in the flat that night, on an uncomfortable rollout camping mattress, in the room with the least amount of dust. I was surrounded by tools, tubes of Grip

Fill and mould-resistant silicone, and circular saw blades freckled with rust.

I ate a takeaway falafel and chips from the local Turkish round the corner, my laptop perched on my lap, using my phone's Internet to search for any experience like the one I'd had that day. I was not a religious man and viewed those with talk of guardian angels and other such things as pathetic and deluded.

But I took a great interest in the stories I found, nonetheless.

I was alone in the flat, peeling off wallpaper in the hallway with a heavy-duty stripping knife I'd bought in B&Q in the Colosseum Retail Park, an area soon set to be demolished to make way for an 1800-home development. I'd accidentally sliced my own hands with the knife several times now – a smear of my own blood had soaked into the exposed plaster, the stain resembling a glyph from an archaic language. I liked how it looked and how the dust settled in the blood.

I'd been doing this for days and knew there was something wrong with my arm. Unused to such stresses, I'd trapped a nerve or pulled a muscle in my right arm during the endless repetitive physical action. Some of the paper would only budge if I put all my considerable weight into it, and all of my strength. I'd been waking up in the middle of the night in agony, my arm on fire like a thin rod of burning metal had been inserted under the skin, stretching from my index finger to my elbow. I tried not to wake Elizabeth as I lay there unable to sleep, whimpering in pain, ashamed of my weakness. Eventually I'd fall asleep again for an hour or two to wake zombie-tired, and have to do it all again. Coffee got me going, and the coke and ibuprofen kept the pain at bay. I tried to eat things like bananas, oat porridge, stuff they said was good for maintaining energy levels throughout the day, but often I had no appetite.

As I worked, I listened to some intense death and grind albums. I was furious with pain and unhappy at how long the project was taking, and the frantic, impossibly intense music matched my mood and reflected my negativity back at me in a way that felt uplifting. I was aware of the arguments around how healthy such music was, but it still meant something to me and had helped me through some difficult times in my life.

The repetitive work allowed me to drift into a nostalgia about my shock at discovering such intense art existing in this grey world. Memories of me and my mate Dan going to underground DIY punk and hardcore shows in tiny basement venues, rooms above pubs, squats, social centres with terrible sound. It was a time when I'd felt the world opening up for me, showing some of its mystery and depth. Things became a lot more complicated and infinitely more exciting.

It had also led me into a world I was now trying to leave. I knew my addictions would get the better of me if I let them. I needed self-control, restraint. The flat, and the future life it represented, would temper my worst impulses.

So, I kept chipping away, getting our new home ready, building our future.

Pain rippled up my arm as I breathed in deep lungfuls of dust.

Two years previous, I had taken an abortive holiday with Elizabeth to the Cotswolds. It was a disaster, and we had not spoken about it since. By then, though some in society could still not admit it, we all knew deep down that the weather had gone wrong. The evidence was everywhere. I tried to keep my views on all this to myself; you couldn't plan a future with someone whilst thinking of towns collapsing into the sea, storms ravaging coastlines, heatwaves rendering large parts of the globe uninhabitable.

What was supposed to be a lovely Spring getaway, romantic, with a chance to walk and explore a postcard-pretty England, was deluged. Violent storms and torrential storms lashed the country, and we huddled in our rented holiday home, unable to go anywhere. We watched films, resenting each other as the incessant rain pounded the windows outside.

I thought about this holiday a lot as I worked on the flat. How the waters would wash all the dust away.

I sat in the garden – my garden, I realised – smoking, watching a few birds argue over the feeder I'd newly installed at the back of the garden.

I was taking a break. I could hear Elizabeth's father and the two lads from Ponders End talk loudly inside, their radio playing pop and rock hits from the 1990s. I knew the words to almost every song.

Magpies chattered noisily on the roof of my neighbours. I saw a goldfinch flit across the garden, chirruping as it went.

There was a time in my life when I would never even have considered this possible. But here I was. At times, I felt like I was hovering over myself and watching a stranger enact the things I had always wanted but never seriously contemplated. Who was this bad actor who wore my face?

I watched a pair of blue tits alight on the feeder, filling themselves with seed.

How many years had it been? A decade and a half stretch I was on it. A party that I never thought would end, though I had wanted it to for years. I had no self-control, with no real motivation to stop what I was doing. That's part of what addiction is, I suppose – the inability to see any reason to stop.

Nights of pounding chests and the fear of a heart attack looming like a vengeful revenant.

Hoarse throats stripped by whiskey, no water, tobacco dry.

Clothes imbued with the stink of stale cigarettes.

Blocked nostrils and bloody tissues floating in a dirty toilet bowl.

White rails leading to nowhere.

Stupid, pointless, repetitive conversations that lasted for years and never were resolved.

All the talk of things we were going to do that sounded plausible at the time and never happened.

Nausea, depression, worthlessness, headaches, regret.

There was always the drink. There was always the powder. Always the dust.

Then I met Elizabeth. I gave myself permission to calm down.

I was taught moderation; learned temperance.

A gust of wind blew through the garden, shaking the branches of the plane tree that grew tall by the back fence. Three magpies shot into the air in alarm. A grey squirrel bolted next door. Dust billowed through the garden, blown from inside the flat. Sawdust and dead skin and fine red brick powder was flung high into the sky.

For a moment, I heard the beating of large, muscular wings. I looked around, but there was nothing bigger than a lone gull, floating high up in the eggshell blue.

Autumn became Winter and the orb weavers disappeared, or died, or whatever they do. The flat was nearly completed, and Elizabeth and I were in good spirits. What had seemed like an impossible and abstract idea was now solidifying rapidly into reality.

The bedroom was complete, and so we now camped out in our own property as we worked decorating the other rooms. It was hard work and tempers occasionally flared, but the work was fulfilling and had a clear goal in sight.

Now she was here, I'd nearly kicked the tobacco and the rest of it. I had a reason, finally, to stop.

One morning, I woke early and decided to go for a run. A lap around the town, cutting through the park, part of my new exercise regime. Get the endorphins up, the blood flowing, all that stuff that other people do. I ran through the Town Park, passing other runners and early-morning dogwalkers, a few buggy-pushers. I wondered if I'd soon be one of them.

By the New River at Gentleman's Row, a local alcoholic who I saw frequently in the area was sat slumped on a bench, despite the cold misty drizzle. It was early, and he still had time before he would inevitably be moved on by the council or police. He was asleep, a can of lager held gently in his left fist, snoring roughly.

I paused for a moment, catching my breath with recovering lungs, taking in the sight of the New River.

Over the water, for a second, I saw a figure with marble skin, eight-foot tall in the morning mist, its wings outstretched like the embracing and comforting arms of a mother. But the vision faded almost as soon as it had appeared, and a huge grey heron that had been standing motionless by the murky waters of the canal took flight.

The air was clean, fresh, dust free. The previous night's rain had washed it all away.

I watched the heron ascend, over the back garden and rooftops of the plush houses that backed onto the waterfront, before disappearing into the mist. The beating of its wings was like a heartbeat.

The man on the bench began to stir with a groan.

I kept running.

The Fool

Carly Holmes

Even before I saw him, the sound of his whining, a low grizzle punctured by high-pitched yips, brought me to my feet and looking around the empty room – *Fool?* – before I remembered. I sank back into my chair, returned my attention to the blank, unforgiving canvas spread before me on its easel. I shook my head at the instinctive, physical tug of longing, jerking it loose, and tried to concentrate on just what was in front of me, swirling Cerulean Blue into Naples Yellow with the delicate tip of a paint brush.

After the creature was silenced with a shout and a heavy, meaty thud of flesh on flesh, the echo of its distress sang in my ears so that I wasn't sure if it was still crying or not. And then the whining started again, was silenced again, moving me through the afternoon in stuttering bursts of brisk anxiety – *Fool?* – and then a sagging remembrance, so that by early evening I was furious with the unseen man, nauseous with despair. I'd destroyed my painting, heaping clots of Cadmium Orange onto the canvas with sudden, heavy-handed desire to produce the perfect auburn, bristling the brush through the mix to recreate the coarse ruff of neck fur. Another ruined painting, another wasted day. If I didn't make more of an effort to concentrate, there'd soon be another disappointed client.

I dropped my phone into the deep pocket of my overall, gathered up coffee mugs and plates heaped with forgotten sandwiches now crisp and curled at their edges, and went downstairs. If I put music on and closed the windows, sat in the back of the house, I could get through the rest of the evening without having to hear that pitiful sound. And in a few hours it would be time for bed; tomorrow I'd phone the council or the police, whoever you were supposed to phone to report these things.

But its wailing trotted at my heels and joined me in the small room I sometimes referred to as my den, sometimes, ironically, my study. It crouched at my feet once I'd settled into my armchair, and whimpered through the light, high rush of the piano. Its howl clung onto the edges of the violin's cadenza, lengthening the notes so that they hung in the air long after they should have ended. I fidgeted for a while, straining to pierce the symphony, searching out the noises that swelled beneath and beyond the music, and then I stood up and silenced the stereo. I walked through to the living room that overlooked the street, standing framed in the long window, sunlit, watching the house opposite. I could see my neighbour's shadow – he'd not long moved in, we'd never spoken – looming as a giant in his garden, striding and then freezing, hunching, bending. There was the occasional metallic clatter of something hitting the ground. I flinched to the side when he emerged through the gate, kicking it wide, his cheeks on fire and swollen with exertion. Dumbbells rolled at his feet. He paused to jab a finger and shout something at the low shape that cowered on the end of a length of rope behind him, then kicked the gate shut and strode off down the road towards the din of shops and pubs, one hand heaving at the waistband of his tracksuit bottoms as they slithered up and down his hips.

The lowering sun was warm and rosy when I stood on my front step and blinked slowly, following the spiralling orange as it blazed beneath my eyelids. A pause before I started walking – was I going to do this again? – but my mind was already on the other side of the road, my body twitching to join it.

I swung my head to the left and then to the right. The residential street was emptied of humans, the dead hour before dinner. I walked down the path to my gate, left it opened wide behind me, and crossed to the opposite pavement. I opened the man's side gate and stepped into his garden – more of a yard, a worn concrete square with no lawn or plants, no shade. Nowhere to hide. The dog cringed onto its back and watched me through screwed-up eyes, shivering its tail.

I bent over it – him – and ran a finger along the long, sensitive ridge of nose, plucked softly at the feathery tip of an ear, then I unbuckled the frayed collar with its filthy knot of rope and laid it on the ground. 'Come on, Fool,' I said, and made a clicking sound with my tongue. I turned and walked back through the gate, across the pavement to the parched strip of grass that bordered the road. I waited for a moment, sure and serene, and when Fool came to stand beside me we crossed together, his flank pressed against my leg. The tiny bones in my neck were brittle with tension, braced for a shout that didn't come. I imagined the rows of windows behind me crowded with people, the entire neighbourhood watching my theft. I didn't look back.

When we reached my side of the street Fool ran ahead of me, gambolling through my gate and up the path as if he'd done it a thousand times before, as if he knew this house was home. He nosed through the flower bed and raised a leg swiftly, marking the fuchsia bush as his. When I pushed the front door open, he slipped past me and veered right, eeling his way through the living room to the kitchen and the water bowl underneath the counter. His padding form flickered fire and smoke as he weaved in and out of sun dapples and deep patchy shade, one moment blazing and the next barely there.

I closed the front door and reached behind me to draw the bolt across while I watched him take a long drink. When he raised his head at last, his soaked muzzle drizzling water onto the floor, he peered round at me. His wide eyes had the colour and shine of virgin conkers before the bruise, still plump on the tree.

'You're a good boy, Fool, yes you are,' I told him, and he dropped his lower jaw to grin at me toothily, narrowing his eyes to slits. I could have pitched forward into that grin, curled up inside its scarlet depths. How I'd yearned for that grin. He raised himself stiffly upright and slid past me again, licking quickly at my hand, and leapt onto the sofa. He tunnelled beneath the cushions, butting them onto the rug, and wriggled himself into a question mark. Sighing softly, he glanced at me again as if for approval or reassurance, and then pocketed his nose into the sharp hollow behind his jutting thigh bone and prepared himself for sleep.

I moved around him, making dinner, writing lists for the things we'd need. All the time trying to be as smooth and quiet as possible so that I didn't disturb his rest. All the time marvelling at his ability to sleep so deeply, a paw flung out and pedalling in rhythm to his dreams, while the man who lived across the road stood on his front step and shouted through the evening, his voice hoarsening more as the hours went by.

When I woke in the night, Fool was stretched out alongside me in the bed, his spine tracing mine. I whispered a few words and he snuffled a response, lifted his tail for one effortful wag. The press of his body, the warmth of it through the thin sheet, was more comfort than I'd had in a long time. It was only now, having him back home, that I allowed myself to feel just how much, how desperately, I'd missed him.

We were in the back garden the next morning, Fool crouched on the untidy lawn at the far end doing his business while I sat in the shade of the apple tree in my pyjamas and drank coffee. I'd need to get his lead from the cupboard under the stairs, take him out for a walk before the day got too warm. It was going to be lovely using it again, buffing the thick blue leather until it gleamed, hanging it from its hook by the coat cupboard.

I watched him meander along the fence, nose in the air as he waded through the long grass. He paused to scent something, moved on again, circled back. The sunlight drenched his fur, glossing him a shade of orange I knew I'd never be able to reproduce at my easel. Had never been able to. And now I felt the familiar compulsion to try anyway, despite the vows not to neglect my commissions, not to compromise my fragile financial security. But that orange. Later, after we'd been out, I'd take his bed up to my studio and paint him as he slept.

Somebody rang the bell of the house next door. A loud questioning voice, my neighbour's quiet response, then a brief silence. I raised a hand to summon Fool to my side, laid a fingertip on his nose to silence any urge to bark. We sat and listened to the bell jangling beside my own door, waited until the letterbox clanged and then the person moved along to the next house. I drained the rest of my coffee in two gulps and we went indoors.

On the mat in the hallway there was a sheet of paper with a blurred photograph of a dog and the word *Zero* beneath it. Missing, believed stolen. Reward for any information. It didn't specify how much of a reward.

'What do you think?' I asked Fool, holding the sheet close to his face so that he could sniff at it. 'Is it a good boy like you?' The image was in black and white, smudged from the man's greasy, clumsy handling. It lacked Fool's tiger stripes, that smouldering camp-fire glow smudged through with reams of charcoal. The missing dog could be any colour, and any size really. Any number of different dogs. But clearly not this dog, not my Fool. I felt sorry for the man, briefly, with his missing pet, clearly a beloved companion, and his sad search.

While Fool ate a bowl of cornflakes soaked in tea, the best I could do with so little in the cupboards, I got dressed and hunted out his collar, spent a while polishing the round identification disc until it shone like a gold coin and the letters of his name stood out bold and proud.

Fool waited patiently outside, sprawled in the shade of the shop awning, while I hurried along the aisles inside and filled my basket with food for us both. Before I queued at the till I went to check on him; he was partly submerged beneath a wave of patting hands and admiring children, his gaze fixed on the doorway with cheerful stoicism. His tail stirred the dust on the pavement when he caught my eye but he stayed where he was, trusting on my return. The fur of his chest was still damp and slightly curled from his swim in the river. I itched to pluck a little of it, lay it across the pale freckled flesh of my wrist and admire it. More russet than peach, the chest fur. More fox than tiger.

I loaded my rucksack and we walked home, meandering slowly along the roads so that he could interrogate every weed. There were posters of the missing Zero taped to lampposts and the side of a bus shelter. We turned into my street and Fool dug his claws into the tarmac to halt us when he discovered a particularly juicy smell. I shuffled my shoulders to shift the weight of the rucksack and let him take his time, loosening the lead so that he could track the scent back and forth while I simply stood and breathed the day in. I watched the man who lived in the house opposite me working his way along a line of parked cars, tucking a sheet of paper beneath every windscreen wiper. He glanced over at us, returned to his task, jerked his head back up sharply and stared.

'Zero,' he said. 'That's my fucking dog.' He released the sheaf of posters, letting them slide from the car bonnet to scatter and flutter around his feet.

I wound Fool's lead around my fist a couple of times, pulled him gently to lean against me. 'I'm sorry?' I said. 'This is my dog.' I smiled blankly and looked away from him, began to walk past.

The man strode into my path and tried to grab my wrist. 'That's my fucking dog,' he repeated. 'I've been looking for him since yesterday.' He fumbled for the lead and I tugged my arm away sharply, stumbling backwards to stay beyond his reach. Beside me, Fool yelped in a high, fractured way. I could feel his body trembling against my leg.

'Don't touch me,' I shouted. 'Keep your hands to yourself.'

A woman loading small children into a car a few houses along paused and watched us. She slid a mobile phone from her handbag and held it up, called to someone out of sight. I tipped my head towards her. 'She's phoning the police,' I told him. 'And she's recording you. So you'd better back off right now.' I stepped away, edging along the pavement, all the time watching him carefully, wondering how quickly I could get my rucksack off and swing it. Sirens sounded in the distance, most likely an ambulance responding to some emergency wholly unrelated to this, but I raised a finger and nodded knowingly. 'That was quick.'

He twisted at his thick waist to scan the road behind us then dropped into a clumsy crouch, holding out a hand to Fool. His knee joints crunched with the effort to support his weight and I wondered how he'd be able to lever himself back to standing. 'Come on boy, come on Zero,' he said pleadingly. 'Give me my dog back.'

Fool bared his teeth in a grimace and clashed them together; strong, pointed canines gleaming the yellowish cream of antique pearls. His auburn ruff rose into a stiff peak of hostility, lending him the look of a hyena. He growled quietly, and for a moment he was unrecognisable to me; a wilder, more savage cousin of the Fool I knew. I dug my fingers into those hackles, working my nails through the fur in a frantic massage, and hushed him.

The woman continued to film us. The siren sounds got nearer.

When he flinched back and dropped his hand in sudden defeat, the man's face was a crumple of confusion and distress. His palm lay weakly across his thigh, creased and pink and vulnerable, soft as the underside of a hedgehog. He squinted blindly into the sun as he tried to find me, to focus on me. He rocked slightly on the balls of his feet, one fist clenched on the ground to keep him balanced while I loomed over him. 'I don't get it,' he said. 'He's never growled at me before.'

'He's not your dog,' I told him gently. 'Look, he doesn't even know you. I'm sorry.'

We left him folded on the pavement behind us and crossed the road, heading for home. When we reached my front gate I glanced back; he was still crouched there, staring after us, shaking his head. The sun lay hot and sticky on the tarmac, the air thick in my lungs. The woman had put her phone away and returned her attention to her family, the little Saturday-morning drama forgotten.

Fool spent the rest of the day dozing on a pile of cushions on the floor of my studio, content to be an artist's model, while I sat behind my easel and tried to capture the exact colour of that handful of fur just above his collarbone.

When he finally woke properly in the late afternoon, lurching to his paws and eyeing me, hopeful for a walk or an early dinner, I was streaked every shade of orange but the right one, sheet after sheet of discarded paper slippery on the floor around my feet. I struggled to keep my frustration a damp and small thing inside me, not let it rear up and get loose. The fault was mine, not his, and anyway, why was it so important anyway to recreate his image in a flattened, one-dimensional form when I had him here in front of me as a living, breathing creature? A miracle returned.

But the signs of my failure were all around the room, months' worth of work lining the walls, painting after painting, propped and hung and listing, abandoned framed and unframed, torn in half and drowned in black paint, rolled into corners when I'd finally kicked them away them after giving up once more.

I called him over to me, snipped a pinch of fur with my scissors, and laid it on the table beside my paintbrushes. There, *that* colour. I'd try again tomorrow.

Though a part of me had been expecting it, bracing for it every time a car pulled up on the street outside, I was still shocked when I opened my front door and saw the policewoman standing on my step. The man from across the road lurked in her shadow, clutching his Lost Dog posters. He surged past her when he saw me, wedging a large foot against mine, bruising my ankle bone, and tried to muscle his way in. I kicked from my side and threw my weight against the solid wood, heaving the door partially closed.

'Zero,' he shouted. 'He's in here somewhere.'

It took both of us to push him back outside and onto my front path, the policewoman embarrassed and wrongfooted, apologising to me while she tried to calm him down. I could hear Fool padding down the hall behind me, wanting to know what the excitement was all about. He thrust his muzzle through the wedge of open door and sniffed the air tentatively, pressed the damp nub of his snooker ball nose into my thigh, and then retreated a few feet. He sank down in the cool, dim hallway and bustled his frame into a rough circle, began to scratch at an armpit.

I refused to let them indoors but agreed to open my door fully, providing the man remained behind the policewoman and didn't speak to me. He stalked up and down the path, scuffing around my flower beds and hissing to himself, while she held a poster at arm's length and studied it, studied Fool – now rigorously investigating beneath his tail – and returned to frowning at the poster.

'It's clearly not him,' I said, tapping the paper. 'See, that dog's ears are much more pointed, and it looks a lot smaller all over. More like a terrier really.' We both looked at Fool, who sighed gustily and gnawed at a paw, ignoring us. I leaned close to the woman. 'He was acting strange earlier today, out on the street,' I confided, rolling my eyes at the man discreetly, 'shouting and grabbing at me. I've never spoken to him before. It's not like we have a history or anything.'

'It's hard to tell much from this image,' she said. 'What's he called? The dog. Do you have proof that you own him?

There have been a lot of thefts lately and we're obliged to check every call we get.'

'Fool.' I clicked my fingers and summoned Fool to my side. 'He clearly knows his name. And I think it's just pedigrees that are stolen, to be honest. He's hardly a pure breed.' I bent to kiss the top of his head swiftly, an apology, then pulled my mobile phone from my pocket. 'Here,' I said, angling it so that she could see the screen, swiping through photographs quickly, 'this is last year in Cornwall. Porthcurno beach. Bit blurry, I know, but he was chasing the gulls. And a couple of years ago when we visited my brother at Christmas. Oh, and early this spring, at the bluebell woods at the other side of town.' I snapped the phone closed, tucked it back into my pocket and shrugged. 'Is there anything else you need? I can try and find his vaccination card but it'll take a while.'

The man came to stand behind the policewoman, craning over her shoulder to look at me. I could smell his spoiled-meat breath and twitched backwards, angling my leg out to the side to keep a barrier between him and Fool. 'Are we done chatting yet?' he asked. 'Can I have my dog back now?' His clutching palm had left a damp stain on the arm of her blouse. She asked him to remove his hand and return to the end of the path. I could see from her face that she disliked him, was trying hard to keep hold of her patience and disguise her distaste.

She bent and patted Fool's neck, twisted his collar so that she could read his name tag. 'You're a very good boy, Fool,' she told him. 'You remind me of a dog I had when I was a girl.' She straightened and nodded at me. 'I think I have all the information I need. Sorry to bother you.' She half turned away but then turned back. 'Make sure you give us a call if you have any trouble.' She swivelled her eyes to the side, indicating the man behind her.

I widened my own eyes and smiled slightly, acknowledging the brief and illicit solidarity, then thanked her and shut the door on them both, sealing me and Fool safely inside.

I could hear the man blustering and protesting out in my front garden, the policewoman replying in clipped tones as she steered him firmly away.

When I woke, the bedroom was thick and deep with night, my brain slow with sleep. Fool was standing at the foot of the bed, facing the door – or was he facing me? – growling. I sat up and flailed a hand out to touch him, reassure him that I was here and all was well. I whispered his name, got hold of his scruff and tried to pull him back to a prone position, but he snapped briefly at me, nothing more than a warning, and leapt onto the floor. He padded over to the window that overlooked the street, nosed through the curtains, and pushed his snarl up against the glass.

I joined him, pulling the curtains aside and peering out. Below me, the man who lived across the street was standing on my low front wall. He waved a bottle when he saw me, tipped his head back and howled at the sky. He upended the bottle into his mouth, losing half of it to his scratchy chin and meaty chest, and pointed up at us. 'There's my boy,' he called. 'There's my Zero. Come on, boy.'

Lights flicked on in the houses either side of mine, casting pockets of warm yellow brightness onto the blanched concrete. A window screeched open and a person leaned out to yell, told the man to get lost or they'd phone the police. The man hurled his bottle up at them, didn't wait to watch it smash over the car in their driveway before he'd stooped and hooked another one from a bag by his feet, brought it to his lips. The unseen person shouted and threw something back, a pillow, which sailed over the man's head and landed on the road behind him.

Swaying, laughing, the man kicked his legs out in a clumsy can-can and lost his balance, toppled backwards onto the pavement. There was a sharp crack, a pause, a glossy spill of blood. His outflung hand jittered, the bottle rolling away from his loosened grip.

The unseen person screamed. Beside me, Fool howled and bit at the window, thrusting himself at the glass as if he could push through it and leap down into the street. I slid onto my knees as if I might be able to hide from the scene outside, thought about tugging the curtains closed and crawling on my hands and knees back to bed, curling my body around Fool's and sleeping through the rest of this night. When I woke in the morning the man would be gone and the mess on the pavement would have been cleaned off.

There were people on the street now, bending over the man, covering him with a blanket, talking loudly. I watched them weaving around each other, barefoot, their faces blank with shock, jawlines and cheekbones harshly angular in the bitter glow of the streetlights. I knelt with my arm around Fool – now quiet and subdued as he leant against me and trembled – and waited until the ambulance had arrived, the police cars, and then I got dressed and went downstairs to answer the knock on the door.

Painting was the only thing that might calm me through the following days, so I threw myself into the process with an intensity that would have made my art lecturer at college proud. Whenever I went outside to walk Fool I kept my gaze levelled on the far distance, moving swiftly along our street to avoid any conversation with my neighbours. I knew they watched me when I passed their houses, and I'd seen them speaking to the police, didn't know what awful things they might have said.

I'd heard that the man from across the road was critically ill but likely to survive, though as a much-reduced version of himself. The thought of that problem now potentially being resolved – no more night-time disturbances or accusations of theft if the man wouldn't even remember he'd once had a dog – should have brought me relief, but I felt nothing other than a queasy disquiet, a despairing sense of everything having been ruined. And Fool seemed depressed, not looking for treats or attention any longer, spending his time at the window or the door as if he were waiting to be let out, or for someone to be let in.

I'd collected several snippets of his fur over the days following the accident and lined them up on my work bench in a procession of orange shades, from darkest rust from his belly through to a small tuft of light apricot I'd found and carefully cut from inside his ear. I held a magnifying glass over the different colours, examining each slowly for hours until they were imprinted on my retinas, staining my vision with their exact hues. But when I began to mix the paint my initial confidence, my sublime belief that this time I would achieve what I needed to achieve, soon dissolved into frustration and panic. I knew the precise orange I wanted, I could see it even when my eyes were closed, yet it eluded me as soon as I wielded my brush with intention.

I got close at times, closer than I'd ever managed before, but never close enough.

It was happening again. It never changed. And though I didn't want to blame Fool, for the blame had to lie with me and my lack of talent, I couldn't help but shun him whenever he eventually left his vigil at the window and came to me for a fuss. I stopped talking to him, merely pointed or snapped my fingers to summon his focus, and the silence saturated every room in the house so that we had to swim through it in order to get from the kitchen to the living room, from the living room to the bedroom. An orange wash of silence that tinged everything and yet never made it onto the paper that lay stretched and waiting on my easel.

On the morning I saw the community ambulance deposit the man in front of his house, watched him walk slowly on crutches to his door and stand there, wavering and unsure, somehow flimsy, before fumbling his key into the lock and shuffling inside, I opened my own front door wide and told Fool to go.

He clung to my ankles for a while, rolled onto his back and grimaced up at me, slunk around me in tight figures of eight. Then he flew through the door and down the path, vaulted the gate and plunged across the road. Heading for home.

He wasn't my Fool. If he had been then he'd have made that leap from room to frame, allowed me to paint him. My Fool was still lost, a blurred image slipping between canvasses in my studio. Still elusive. But getting closer to home.

I focussed entirely on my commissions, soothed angry customers who had expected better from me, and found a tranquillity once again in landscapes and still life.

The man across the road walked his dog twice a day, limpingly and slowly, muttering to it or himself quietly the whole time. He stopped frequently to rest, leaning on a stick that he always carried with him. He stared at the world around him vaguely as if not quite sure where he was, whether he belonged here. If I passed him, he nodded briefly but didn't speak. I wondered if he struggled with forming words. I wondered if he had any memory of standing on my front wall, shouting at me, accusing me of theft.

The dog, Zero it was called, never once pulled on his leash when it saw me, never stopped to greet me. I might have thought at one time that it looked like my Fool but I could see now that it didn't.

I started a new commission, my most important yet. This one could pay the mortgage for the next six months. I settled myself back into my usual routine, sat every day and frowned at the vast, stern spread of white that was my immediate future. I began to paint.

The sound of whining, a low grizzle punctured by high-pitched yips, brought me to my feet and looking around the empty room – *Fool?* – before I remembered. I sank back into my chair, returned my attention to the canvas spread before me on its easel. I shook my head at the instinctive, physical tug of longing, jerking it loose, and tried to concentrate on just what was in front of me, swirling Cerulean Blue into Naples Yellow with the delicate tip of a paint brush. The tube of Cadmium Orange lay just beyond my pot of water.

And then the whining started again, was silenced again, moving me through the afternoon in stuttering bursts of brisk anxiety – *Fool?* – and then a sagging remembrance. I walked to the window that overlooked the back gardens of this terrace of houses, opened it wide and leaned out into the rain. A few houses down from me, partly obscured by an early dull dusk and overgrown shrubs, I could make out a creature slinking along the soiled strip of grass that was its entire world. It shivered in the cold air, its fur soaked through and plastered to its skinny frame.

Even from this distance and through the haze of rain and twilight, I could see it gleamed a rich, autumnal orange. 'Fool?' I called.

He turned his head and looked at me.

The Chariot

Malcolm Devlin

Here she is. Annie alone in a dark room. Her feet are under her on the couch, a cushion propped behind her back. The television is on, the sound is down, the light of it plays across her face and hands, bands of colour her eyes do not meet. In her hand is her phone and on its screen a different image holds her attention.

Here she is. Little Lisa, measured only in months and asleep in a gauzy glow in the room upstairs. She lies with her head to one side, her arms up, her feet down. A roughly drawn capital H, a K, an X; here Roman, then oblique. Her face is serious in her dream and Annie has an urge to reach into her phone and gently smooth the frown line away before it sets.

She watches as though she might see Lisa move. Stillness frightens her sometimes, astonishes her at others. She looks closely at the fat square pixels in that hope she might see them blink as her little girl breathes. She imagines the motors and engines of her, moving with an independence she has no part of.

She watches, and the act of watching makes her feel obscene. But there she is, hoping, fearing she might witness her daughter grow.

A notification slides down the screen, obscuring the view. Thomas is calling, still at work. Annie is frustrated she cannot answer the phone and watch Lisa at the same time.

"Hello?"

"Annie. I'm sorry. Are you asleep?"

His phone is crooked, she can only see ceilings. He's walking, his face appears and disappears from the corner.

"No. The lights are off. I was watching a film."

"What are you watching?"

She doesn't remember. She looks to the screen. Bright faces. Bright colours. Sandals. Dust.

"Just a film."

"How's Lisa?"

"Asleep."

"Bless her."

He says this as though only their daughter has learned how to sleep. Perhaps it's true. He works nights, Annie works days. They take Lisa in shifts until she settles.

The view of the ceiling crosses into somewhere dark. A fluorescent light flickers into too-brightness and the phone dips, controls itself.

Here he is. Thomas. Neat and trimmed, his uniform suit buttoned up tight. She recognises the cupboard he has hidden himself in. It's a linen store and she knows exactly which linen store it is. It's the one on the second floor and it doesn't look as though it has changed since she worked at the hotel all those years ago. It still has that same pink plastic pig toy tied to the end of the light cord; it swings behind Thomas's head, its dopey expression photobombing him with each pass.

"Is everything alright?" She's impatient to return to the video feed. Little Lisa, moving, unmoving.

"Yes. Yes. I was just taking a break. Just checking in."

"I'm fine. We're fine."

"Good. Good."

The conversation stalls. She wonders if he was hoping for something more dramatic. An excuse to come home. An excuse to leave her to cope on her own.

"Is everything okay at the hotel?"

"Everything's fine."

"Busy?"

"No. Quiet night. So far."

"Same. Same. So far."

"Nothing happened."

"No, nothing happened."

They dwindle. On the television a race is starting. Crowds cheer in silence, horses sweat and paw the dirt. A blur of movement and adrenaline, a crash that – even muted – feels too loud. She finds the remote and presses pause.

"I've got to go," Annie says. "She's starting up."

It's a lie but she almost believes it.

"She'll be fine."

"I've got to go."

Lisa is fine. Lisa is asleep. The bedroom looks warmer in person than the alien tinge of the night vision camera, a honey-glowing nightlight in the shape of a rabbit sits beside the crib. Lisa pouts, her eyes balled up, and Annie stands over her, struck again by the sheer wonder of her.

And she's entranced again. Just as she was by the image on her phone. A live performance of the same routine.

And then...

Chariot.

Annie catches her breath.

Chariot.

Now, then. Where did that come from? A memory, of course. It's been circling in the far distance since Lisa was born. A shadow chasing her across the walls, a blur of shape and volume, hunting for the right, arbitrary trigger to bring itself into focus and make itself inescapable. Why now? Why here? Annie steps back. Too quick, she stumbles and the sound of her misplaced footfall makes her freeze as though the simple act of *remembering* might wake the girl. Lisa sleeps, undisturbed. Her mother backs catlike out of the bedroom, refusing to let her memory and her daughter occupy the same limited space.

"Chariot."

Here they are. Annie and Thomas, together but not yet *together*. This was... how many years ago? Thomas would remember. It was where they met, but not where they *met* and that's a distinction that seems important when sorting the knots of the past. Thomas records everything with his schedules and planning meetings and endless notes and reminders. Annie has always been happy to coast. In this memory, for example, he is running his finger down the ledger, showing her a name. The scene feels so fresh to her, it may as well also exist in the present tense.

"Charlotte?"

"Chariot. Although... it's the same. I think. French, maybe?"

They stand behind the reception desk of the Causeway Inn – nowhere near a causeway and not really an Inn. It's a service station hotel chain on the outskirts of the city, surrounded by an arabesque of A-roads and motorways.

Annie and Thomas are wearing matching waistcoats and pinstripe shirts. Their heads are bowed inwards examining the same document. A line written in Thomas's hand, *Mr and Mrs Julian Morris*. His fingertip rests on the suffix, *plus child*.

"But. Chariot? Like—"

"I know! Poor kid. Maybe five. Maybe six. Looked mortified as she followed them down the hall. *Chariot*, the dad goes. *Come on Chariot.*"

Evening is approaching, the shifts are turning. Just Annie tonight in this wing, Thomas is about to leave. Outside, the traffic has thinned from a constant roar to an intermittent clap of thunder. Thomas talks her through who has arrived, who is due, what to look out for. For the next six of her full eight hours she'll have one-hundred-and-sixteen rooms and the sixty-four guests who are stying in them all to herself.

"Room 212. Just flown in and still jet-lagged. I told them we'd keep the bar menu open for them."

"The bar menu?" Annie is still green. She doesn't like the idea of being by herself on the night desk. Every responsibility balanced on her shoulders alone seems to make the corridors longer and the darkness pressing against the windows a little blacker than it should be.

"You just need to heat things up. You know how it goes. Zap it in the oven. Follow the instructions. It's only them. You'll be fine."

She *will* be fine. His smile is faintly patrician. He's been working here longer than she has. Older, not by much, but enough for her friends to talk. Tonight at least, his diligent experience trumps her ambition to be somewhere else. Perhaps she even respects that.

"If anything happens, you have my number. But nothing will happen."

"Nothing will happen."

The phone goes half an hour after he does. It's half-past-eleven and the voice is reedy and indistinct. It sounds like the sort of voice she might expect to hear recorded on an ancient wax cylinder, yet here it is ordering chicken nuggets from the children's menu and two portions of lasagne with side salads.

Annie finds the food easily, the bar menu is limited for a reason. She heats it easier still and marvels at how the details she frets about most prove to be the least troublesome when the hour arrives. She stacks the trolley and rattles it in the lift to Room 212.

The man who opens the door is younger than she was expecting. Not *young* young, but not old old either. The voice she heard on the phone is a strange fit to his face. He has an old fashioned hair parting and spindly glasses, but his smile is expansive as he opens the door wide to allow her inside.

The room is every room in the Causeway Inn. A double bed with a single bunk built across it. A dressing table, an uncomfortable chair, a window that doesn't open and has no view. The woman sitting on the bed is younger than the man by a clear and vivid margin. She is closer to Annie's age. Twenties to his fifties, she is barefooted and bedheaded and the oversize T-shirt she wears as a nightshirt is pulled down to cover the knees she hugs close to her chest. The expression she gives Annie simmers with resentment. A stranger in the room. A private bubble burst.

Annie fusses with the plates, distracted by numbers that don't add up. How old is he? How old is she? How old is the little girl? *Where* is the little girl? Neither the man nor the woman speak or move to help and the silence is rough like sandpaper. Annie offloads the food as neatly as she can onto the dressing table but she feels faintly tainted by the couple's proximity. Cutlery wrapped in napkins. Cruet in paper sachets. Two bottles of water and a raspberry Fruit Shoot. When she straightens, the toilet in the ensuite flushes, the door opens and another woman steps through. This woman is older, closer in age to the man with grey in her hair and wearing the same reined-in weariness across her face. When the older woman thanks her, Annie realises it was she who made the phone call and not the man, but her sense of disorientation is compounded by mathematics. Three adults in the room and yet... *Plus child*, she thinks. *Five or six*, she thinks. *Poor kid*, she thinks.

She wants to say something but she doesn't know what. She knows that none of the questions she has lining up inside of her would survive ridicule spoken aloud.

It's the man who speaks first, and he doesn't speak to Annie. He lifts the plate of chicken nuggets to the young woman's face as though the chemical smell might jolt her out of her apathy.

"There. Are you hungry? Look, it's your very favourite."

It's the emphasis he uses that makes Annie frown before she considers the words themselves. There's a strange enthusiasm to *look*; a contrived playfulness to *hungry*; a heightened quality to *very*.

"And a *Fruit Shoot*. You *adore* Fruit Shoots."

To her credit, the young woman looks nonplussed. She looks past the proffered goods and regards Annie with a look that might also be an accusation.

The man snaps his fingers.

"Chariot. Look at me."

Chariot.

The young woman looks to the man, tired, but awake enough to fashion her silent insolence into something sharp. The man glances at Annie, stress-lines fracturing his smile.

"Was there something else?"

There's desperation there, but that's not why Annie backs away. It sounds like he's saying something she should be saying. *Can I help you with anything else, sir?* Any authority she once possessed has fractured. Three adults, two paid for. Is this fraud? Theft? What? She should *say* something. She should *do* something. Again, the dislocation makes her weightless.

The trolley rings as she kicks it with her heel.

"Excuse me."

The older woman doesn't push past her, she's too polite, too middle class for that. She *steps* past her, gently moving Annie out of the way with firm and papery hands. For the briefest moment, Annie has a sense she is being herded towards the door. The three of them, together against the one of her, feel vast.

She wants to leave, but she doesn't want to leave everything unspoken because if she carries the questions out with her, they might thicken into something unmanageable. She clears her throat.

"The bar's closed but if you'd rather I brought another lasagne, there's plenty."

Weak. She should confront them. Berate them. Knowing that Thomas would know what to do makes it worse. They're taking her for a fool and she's allowing it.

The older woman regards her with an endearing confusion. Annie clarifies.

"I just meant the children's portions are very small and—"

"Well."

The bemusement shared between the older man and the older woman softens into a kind condescension.

"She *is* only five."

The young woman turns to Annie, her expression dark. *Obviously*, her face says. Her attention is like sunburn.

Annie moves to say something, anything, but the older woman gets there first. Her arms are up, she's herding again.

"It's late. We should eat. We should get to bed. It's well past her bedtime, I'm sure you understand."

"Absolutely."

There's a keenness in the woman's eyes as she says it, as though she's searching for something.

Annie doesn't understand – this Annie doesn't yet have Lisa, if Lisa might be considered a comparison. This Annie doesn't understand a better way to respond. She allows herself to be ushered out of the room. The younger woman watches every move she makes. Her head angles so she can see better as the door closes and her view narrows and narrows and then extinguishes with a click.

She doesn't call Thomas as soon as she's back at the reception desk. She *wants* to, but even that feels like defeat.

In the present-present, Annie – still standing by Lisa's cot – wonders if the Thomas she wanted to speak so desperately then is the same Thomas she knows now. They look the same, but one she knows from more angles; one she now knows in silhouette as well as bright in the hours before dusk. She's seen him morose in the morning, wounded at weekends; she's seen him laugh in an unguarded way – far removed from the professional amusement he'd reserve for the guests' awful jokes at their expense.

Most of all, she knows him with Lisa. His gentle patience when she screams as though they're equally fresh to the world's strangeness. She envies him sometimes when she sees Lisa look at him for a reassurance that her reality will right itself after a squall, and Annie wonders if it's because she used to look at him in the same way. Behind the reception desk, this sweet, silly little man, in his pinstripes and spectacles. How did he see her back then? Someone young and silly? Someone easy? Someone to take under his benevolent wing?

When did she first *see* him? And when did he start to fade?

"It was a little girl."

Here he is again, past-present Thomas, the voice on the reception desk phone, clear as it ever was. It's nearly one in the morning but he doesn't sound as though he's tired, let alone asleep.

"How little?"

"Five? Six?"

"She seemed older."

"Kids sometimes seem older."

"Eighteen? Twenty?" Her voice is small.

She can tell he's taking the time to regroup and when he speaks again, she can hear how incredulity has been delicately tempered from his reply.

"The father was carrying her. She was asleep, a little bundle in his arms. When he put her down, she tried to reach the counter but couldn't. Stood on her tiptoes."

She says nothing. There's nothing she feels she can say that won't incriminate her further.

"She's just a girl, Annie."

Girl. It's true, she is, but when does a girl cease to be a girl and start to be seen as a woman? At what age is the threshold where the word is no longer appropriate?

"I made a mistake." She hangs up before he can say anything else. She hangs up so fast, she's not even certain he hears her apologise as the phone hits the cradle. She hopes he doesn't.

The night continues, hour after hour. She tries not to think about the family in Room 212, but she assumes that simply knowing they're *there* and that they're *wrong* will hang over her like a canopy, casting shadows on every other thought. But the night proves busy enough that – for a time – she forgets.

She forgets long enough that, stepping out of the lift in the East wing corridor in the pursuit of a minor errand, she almost doesn't realise she's not alone.

Here she is. The young woman, the girl, *Chariot*, standing like a pantomime spectre in the darkness at the far end of the corridor.

The presence of the figure, there in the communal space, takes Annie by surprise. The recognition comes a moment later, a merciless plunge of freezing water.

The girl – let's call her a girl, for brevity's sake – looks the same as she did. Eighteen, twenty, something like that. Her posture is late-teen, surliness, awkwardness and blunted spite. She's still wearing her oversized t-shirt, her hair hanging lank and travel-greased around a pale face.

"Can I help you?"

It's only once she's said it that it occurs to Annie it's not something she would have said had she found an actual child alone in the hotel.

The girl looks up at her; eyes hooded. She doesn't move closer, she steps back, deeper into the shadows.

"I'm lost." It's the first time Annie has heard her voice and it isn't what she expects. It's small, fragile, faintly contrived.

"You're lost." Annie isn't sure if she has the patience for this charade anymore. "You're in Room 212, do you know where that is?"

A short, curt shake of the head. Dark locks flail.

Annie falters in the process of giving the girl directions. She wants to be done for the night. She wants to go home, but she foresees a tangle of frustration that will mire her further if she doesn't tread lightly.

"I'll show you. It's not far."

Now the girl approaches her. Coy, but with quick little footsteps that shuffle on the polyester carpet. When Annie turns, she is surprised to feel a hand curl into her own. It is cool and slick and ever so slightly sticky.

Annie surprises herself by resisting the urge to pull herself free. She glances to her side and sees the girl is her height, perhaps taller. The hand is an *adult* hand, she is certain now there is no mistake.

"Was there something you were looking for?"

She is doing her best to sound diplomatic. Her modulation employing that professional service-industry cadence that treats adults as though they are children.

The girl doesn't answer straight away. When she does, her voice is hesitant. A mumble. Words tumbling over each other to formulate an excuse.

"There was a machine," the girl says. "We saw it on the way in. It was a food machine. Chocolate bars and crisps and liquorish shoelaces. And I had left over pocket money. Look."

Her other hand opens and a small collection of coins shift in the palm. Annie glances at them, their denominations don't quite register. They look foreign. Ill-fitting for the hotel's vending machines.

The childishness of the confusion still feels unconvincing to her. It feels theatrical, as though the girl is overplaying her part.

"Well," Annie says. "Let's get you back to your room."

The girl tugs her arm.

"But the machine," she says.

"I'm sure you can find better things to spend your money on." She's surprised to find herself sounding so school-marmish. She promises herself she'll never sound like that if she ever has children of her own.

Whatever her tone, it seems to have worked. The girl lapses into silence and walks along with her, her fist closed over the coins once more.

The second-floor corridor feels endless, the carpet noisier underfoot. When they reach the door to Room 212, Annie reaches to touch the lanyard where her swipe key is tucked but the girl is faster, she has a key of her own.

"Are your parents asleep?"

The girl looks at her and opens the door and holds it wide.

There's something about this gesture that Annie doesn't like. There's something about the light in the girl's eye.

Annie doesn't mean to look inside the room. She certainly doesn't mean to step inside, but having done the former without care, she cannot help herself but do the latter.

Room 212 has changed since last she was here.

There is the smell of something slightly too sweet, there is a humidity that feels unseasonal. The lights are off, but no room in The Causeway Inn is entirely dark. Not with the halogen lights of the carpark outside bathing everything in their indefinite amber sunset; not with the glow-in-the-dark light fittings and the constellation of LED pilot lights on the television, the kettle, the alarm clock. Within the dusk of the unlit room, it first looks as though the furniture has been disappeared and *something* else has been built in its place. Some monstrous henge in silhouette, something jarring and strange. But no, as her eyes adjust it's clear that everything has simply been stripped clean and moved to a new location. The beds have been dismantled; their constituent parts pushed upright against the far walls. They're anchored in place by the upturned desk and the dressing tables. The bedclothes have been draped across them and the structure now resembles a Beduin tent with a brutalist bent.

Within its canopy, all three of the room's mattresses have been gathered and upon them, the older couple lies side-by-side. Together, but not *together*. They look as though they've been laid out in parallel. On their stomachs, unclothed, their faces turned due west. The stillness of them is frightening but astonishing and Annie has to stare at them closer than she would like to see the glistening skin of their backs rise and fall.

Breathing.

Alive.

Arranged.

The girl pushes past her. The state of the room does not concern or surprise her. Now she's inside, she seems fey, unmoored. Her arms extend and her head tilts back. She turns around the space as though it's a dance floor.

"So silly," she says. "They didn't know I was gone," Her voice still sing-song, but to Annie's ear, the childishness has fractured around the edges.

Annie finds her own voice. "Are they alright?" Of all the things she could say, she's oddly proud to have thought of others first.

The girl doesn't look at her.

"They sleep so deeply. So deeply," she says. She crouches in front of the older couple, her head cocked, animal-like. "Every night they fall into a deep, deep well."

She turns back to Annie.

"You can stay if you'd like," she says, and the smile she gives is lopsided with hope.

"Stay?"

"We can play. They won't wake up. *I'm* not sleepy, are you?"

The girl stands up and turns away again. With a clumsy movement, she pulls the T-shirt she's wearing up and over her head. The fabric rucks up across her shoulders and she has to bend double to free it. When she stands, even in the half-light, Annie sees how her back is scrawled from nape to coccyx. A tattoo applied over the shoulder with felt-tip pens. A blind scribble of coiled lines and indistinct shapes and stunted marks. When she turns back to Annie, she is as naked as the older couple and her eyes are wild.

"Stay," she says again but Annie can barely hear her.

Annie doesn't know where to look.

The girl is by no means five or six. *Surely?* No. Older. Much older. *Clearly?*

Annie steps back, alarmed that the door has been closed behind her. She feels as though she has stepped out of the world. She feels as though she has transgressed over a line she didn't see. The door handle levers down but doesn't open. Her hand flails for the latch she didn't know had been thrown.

"Stay," the girl says. She's turned her back on Annie again, stepping lightly onto the mattresses between the older man and the older woman. The springs give lightly beneath her weight, enough for the man to loll a fraction. His head tilts up and Annie sees his eyes are open, wide and liquid. He stares at Annie from across the room. Behind him, the girl lowers herself down onto the bed, and from Annie's perspective it looks as though she is sinking into the shadows themselves.

Annie's hand can't find the latch. The geography of the door is somehow alien to her, slick and sticky, swelling in the heat.

"Don't you think it's strange?" the girl says. "Everyone you've ever met, everyone you know, every stranger you've ever passed in the street. Don't you think it's strange that everyone you know began *inside* someone else?"

Annie doesn't see the girl again, but she feels *seen* by her. She doesn't know how she gets back in the corridor. She only knows that she hides in the linen closet on the second floor for what feels like hours, watching the plastic pig toy swing back and forth on the light cord, before she finally breaks free and runs all the way back to the reception desk.

Every time the phone rings, every time a door opens somewhere deep in the building, she imagines the girl to be there.

"Nothing happened."

A promise. A prayer. A rehearsal for how she'll explain. But when the morning shift arrives, Annie flees without saying a word. The following day, when she asks, tentatively, about the family in Room 212, the answer is unexceptional to anyone except her.

"A young family. A little girl. Still tired from the flight."
A little girl.

When she summons up the courage to venture to Room 212 she finds it is – again – exactly like every room at The Causeway Inn. Bed, chair, dresser, all in the right places.

"Nothing happened."

A threat. An omen. A shadow she knows will follow her.

And now, and yet, years later, here she is. Annie, in the present-present. Standing once again in the bedroom, her daughter stirring in the crib before her.

How did she get from there to here? Annie? How did she end up with Thomas? When did she leave the Causeway Inn? Is she happy? Is she *really* happy? So many stories get eclipsed along the path. So many stories blotted out by the sudden brightness of those we find along the way.

Here she is. Little Lisa. Eyes wide and sparkling like polished pebbles, all the expressions she's ever had running across her face, too busy to settle.

Annie reaches down and scoops her up. The weight surprises her, it always does. She feels the mass of her daughter in her knees, across her back, in the ache of her arms and neck and she welcomes every screaming nerve signal as though the promise of each might bring them closer.

Lisa's smile breaks like a sunburst. Vast and undisciplined, it demands reciprocation in kind.

"Let's take you downstairs," Annie says.

A beautiful child. *Such* a beautiful child. Of course she is and of course she should think so and yet... sometimes Annie makes the mistake of wondering if others see what she sees. How is Lisa seen now she's a baby? How will she be seen when Annie is no longer there to frame her?

To be seen is such a delicate thing, Annie thinks. Seeing is such an invasive act. What if someone careless sees her without thought? What if someone sees her in the wrong way?

Downstairs, the television is still on, the film paused and glowing. A chariot lies on its side, its wheel broken. A vehicle, treated recklessly and then discarded in the sand and the dust.

The pencil outline of an unwelcome thought intrudes, but before it can fully form, Lisa makes a sound. A low and gentle murmur and like a spell, the idea is gone, the past with it, the film as well. There is only the perfect present, there is only Annie and Lisa and nothing else in the whole world.

"Here she is," Annie says and when the girl smiles, her smile is ageless.

The Tower

Alison Moore

The grown-ups hated the tower block, which cast its long shadow over the houses, sinking the back rooms into gloom. From time to time, a rumour went round that this eyesore, this carbuncle, had been condemned and was to be demolished, but nothing ever happened; it remained standing.

The children had been told quite clearly that they were not to play in the tower block, but they could not seem to stay away.

With the summer stretching on and on and with nothing to do, Julia followed Tilly and Sally over the expanse of cracked tarmac that lay between home and the tower block. Julia kept stopping to look in the cracks, hoping to see an abyss, finding only shallow pits stuffed with cigarette ends. She kept having to run to catch up with the others, her flip flops slapping, echoing off the tower block.

If they stood at the foot of the tower block and looked up, its proportions seemed grotesque. It gave Julia vertigo; it made her feel sick.

The door was never locked. They could just let themselves into the lobby, where they stood around, giddy with the thrill of being out of bounds but unsure what to do with themselves, with their uncertain freedom. It was like waiting for something but not knowing what.

It was cold in there, in their summer clothes. Sally turned herself upside down and walked around on her hands, her bare legs up in the air like tentacles. Tilly pressed the button to bring down the lift, but nothing happened.

Her shorts had deep pockets, full of stuff; she liked to be prepared. She had a little notepad in there, and a pencil stub, and a tube of wine gums which she shared around. Sally dropped onto her feet again, and inspected the filth on her hands before taking a sweet. Tilly said, 'We'll do dares.'

On the first page of her notepad, Tilly wrote, *I saw what you did*. She tore it out and gave it to Sally, and dared her to post it through the door to one of the flats. They all went together up to the first floor, noisy on the bare concrete steps in the echoing stairwell, sniggering and shushing. There was a brass handrail, covered in fingerprints from all the people who went up and down. Julia's mum would say, *Think of the germs*, but Julia had already touched it.

The corridor had a strange smell which Sally said was like vegetables and Tilly said was like the school canteen. Julia said they were breathing in molecules of the residents' dinners and pretended to gulp them down, and then Tilly said the smell was also the particles that came from their bodies, and Julia tried to hold her breath but it was too late anyway.

As soon as the note was through the door, Tilly and Sally ran off up the next flight of stairs, and Julia hurried after them. She remembered climbing an old tower whose stone staircase had no barriers – no railings, not even a guiding handrail – and which gave way to a sheer drop. She had felt frightened but she had kept climbing.

When Julia reached the landing and caught up with her giggling friends, Sally had the pad and pencil and was writing *Everyone thinks you smell*. She gave the note to Julia to post through a door. Julia felt bad about it, but she still did it.

Up on the next floor, Julia was given the notepad, and thought for a while before writing neatly, *You have a secret admirer*. Tilly rolled her eyes. She pushed it through the nearest door and said, as they scarpered up the stairs, 'I dare you to knock.'

'I don't want to knock,' said Julia. 'Someone might answer.'

'You knock and run,' said Tilly. 'We'll all do one.'

Tilly chose their doors. Julia, standing outside hers, said, 'But mine's further from the stairs than yours. I'm more likely to get caught.' She turned her head to look at her friends, as they banged on their doors. 'Wait,' said Julia, as they ran. She raised her own hand and knocked quickly. In an instant, the door opened, as if by magic, or as if someone had been standing there, waiting.

The man in the doorway was older than anyone Julia had ever known, and insanely tall. He was dressed half for indoors and half for going out, in stripy pyjama trousers and fingerless gloves. He looked at her with narrowed eyes and said, 'Yes.'

His door had a peephole in it, and Julia wondered what she looked like through it; she wanted to look through the peephole and see what he saw.

'I saw you coming,' he said.

He couldn't have done, thought Julia; given the angle of his door, there was no way he could have looked through the peephole and seen them coming up the stairs or along the corridor.

'I can see your house from up here,' he said.

Julia wanted to see her house from the man's window, to see what her home looked like from the tower block, but she knew she shouldn't go into his flat. At least, she decided, she should not stay long.

'We're so high up,' said Julia.

The man, standing beside her at the big window, said, 'I like the view from here.'

Julia could see the roof of her house, and the top of her mum's head. Her mum was standing on the back doorstep, maybe looking for Julia. The tower block's shadow was creeping towards the back door.

'They're going to demolish the tower block,' said Julia. 'One of these days.'

'I don't know where I would go,' said the man.

Julia shrugged. 'You'd just have to find somewhere else.'

'Maybe someone would take me in,' said the man.

Julia turned away from the window and said, 'I've got to go now.'

'Don't go yet,' said the man. He moved to a sofa in the living area and patted the seat beside him. Julia moved towards the living area but did not sit down. 'When you die,' said the man, 'would you want to be buried?'

'What?' said Julia.

'When you die,' repeated the man, 'would you want to be buried?'

'I don't know,' said Julia. 'I haven't thought about it.'

'I wouldn't like it,' said the man. 'I wouldn't like to be cremated either.'

'No,' said Julia. But what else was there?

In front of the sofa on which the man was sitting, there was a coffee table, and on the coffee table was a biscuit tin. There was a picture on the lid: the custard creams and pink wafers made Julia's mouth water. The man reached for the tin with his long arms and pulled it towards him. One of his hands was missing two fingers: the fingerless glove had two empty holes. 'Do you want to see what's in here?' he asked, seeing Julia looking.

Julia shifted her gaze from his hand. 'Is it biscuits?' she said.

'No,' said the man, 'it's not biscuits.' He lifted the lid of the tin, and Julia looked inside. He was right: it wasn't biscuits. Her mum kept a dish of sweets on their coffee table, but it wasn't sweets either. She could see hair: wispy strands coiled like a pig's tail, and a fat hank of greying hair tied with a ribbon. The man himself was quite bald. He said to Julia, 'Does your mother have a lock of your baby hair?'

'I don't think so,' said Julia, who thought it would be strange anyway, to have a little bit of her soft baby self, her organic self, kept for years in a box, getting old.

'Well, a lock of baby hair can be valuable,' said the man. 'You've heard of John Steinbeck? A curl of his baby hair was found in a warehouse and put up for auction.'

'Why would you want his hair?' asked Julia.

'An intimate keepsake provides a powerful connection to a person,' said the man. 'I bet your mother has your baby teeth,' but Julia didn't know about that. He unwrapped a tissue-wrapped package that turned out to be teeth of all kinds: small, white teeth; large, yellow teeth; teeth with holes and fillings. 'When Galileo died, his devotees made off with not only a tooth but his fingers. Such things are more than keepsakes; they're talismanic. Einstein's eyes were kept by his eye doctor, who said having them *means that the professor's life has not ended. A part of him is still with me.* They're in a safe deposit box in New York, and may yet come to auction. People pay a lot of money for such intimate items. Winston Churchill's false teeth sold for thousands of pounds. Sylvia Plath's tarot cards sold at auction for six figures. A perfectly ordinary pack of cards, and not even pristine: one of them, the Tower card, was discoloured, either from being in sunlight or from being too close to the fire. A hundred and fifty thousand pounds because they were *hers*. Tarot cards pick up the energy of the person using them. They're deeply personal items, which makes them so valuable.'

Julia did not like the thought of tarot cards, as if, like a Ouija board, using them could make something happen, and it would be something bad.

'These things,' he said as he rewrapped the teeth, 'are sacred relics.'

Julia knew all about sacred relics. She told him she had seen Saint Genevieve's finger bone in a glass case in a French church. The rest of her had been lost in the French Revolution.

'Those relics from the saints and the martyrs are believed to have healing powers,' said the man. 'Life-giving properties. In God's kingdom, what is broken will become whole again. Even a finger bone would have power.'

Julia thought of Roald Dahl's Magic Finger and the havoc it could wreak, and it crossed her mind that this was a good reason for keeping Saint Genevieve's finger behind glass, locked away, where it could do no harm.

'Even today, they're traded online,' said the man. 'Strands of hair and fragments of bone, centuries old. It's a violation of the rules – the rules of eBay, the rules of the Church – but it still happens.'

It was a grim thought, old bits of bone and hair, remnants of ancient bodies, coming through the post. 'What if you're not getting what you think you are?' asked Julia. 'What if you're just getting any old hair, any old bones?'

'You could be,' said the man, 'but I know what I have: everything in here is my own – my hair, my teeth.'

Julia said again, 'I've got to go now.'

'Go then,' replied the man, putting the lid back on the tin. 'I'm not stopping you.'

Julia let herself out and ran home. It was later than she'd realised and she was ready for her supper. She might have Sugar Puffs, sitting at the kitchen table. But then again, she thought, remembering the view from the man's window, she might not.

Julia sat quietly on her bed, just waiting for it to be over.

'*Anything* could have happened,' said her mum.

'I'm fine,' insisted Julia. 'Nothing happened.'

'But it *could*,' said her mum, glaring through the window at the vast grey slab of the tower block. 'You can stay in here and think about what you've done.' She turned away, leaving Julia to her punishment. 'You bring it on yourself,' she added before closing the door. Her slippered feet retreated, though her anger remained in the air.

Julia hated being grounded, and there was never any limit to it; her grounding was indefinite, until her mum said otherwise. She could not even talk to Tilly or Sally, though she was not sure she wanted to; it was her friends who had snitched on her, who had told the grown-ups that she had gone into the man's flat.

She looked across at the tower block, at its grid of windows, one of which was his. If she were to look through binoculars, she might be able to work out which one, but she was afraid she would see him looking back at her.

She could smell the brass handrail. She kept bringing her hand to her face and sniffing at the palm, at the tang still clinging to her skin.

She lay back on her bed and looked up at the ceiling, at the patterns in the stucco. If she looked hard enough, she could see faces.

There were birds on her windowsill. They came for the crumbs she put out there, though she wasn't supposed to, and now they came even when she hadn't put anything out.

Julia did not get her supper, and was only allowed out of her room to use the bathroom, but the following day she was permitted to come downstairs for meals. Her mother kept her at home until the end of the summer holidays, and then Tilly and Sally called for her on the way to school and Julia returned to the world.

'But you're not to go back there,' said her mum, letting her go.

'I don't want to go back there,' said Julia, who didn't ever want to see the man again.

At the weekend, they went back to the tower block.

They were still in their summer clothes but it was colder now, and the lobby was draughty in a way Julia had not noticed before. Sally cartwheeled from one side of the lobby to the other, not caring about the dirt on her hands. Tilly pressed the lift buttons, not expecting anything to happen. When the door slid open, they all just looked at it, and then Tilly said, 'Come on, then.'

They rode up and down playing chicken, taking turns pulling awful faces each time the lift door opened, but there was never anyone there, and after a while, Tilly said, 'Let's do dares.'

'I'm not doing knock and run,' said Julia, as the lift stopped on a floor of Tilly's choosing. They exited into a hallway, closed doors stretching ahead on either side. All the hallways looked the same, except for the numbers on the doors. Julia tried to remember the number of the tall man's flat but she had not been paying attention; she didn't even know which floor his flat had been on. She remembered his peephole, but every one of these doors had a peephole. It was so hard to tell them apart – the doors, the floors.

She had told her friends about the biscuit tin and what was in it; she had described the locks of hair. Her friends said they were probably trophies, like serial killers keep. No, said Julia, it was his own hair, he had said so, but they had jokes about it now, about the weird man's biscuit tin.

'I don't want to do knock and run,' insisted Julia.

'You can knock and *not* run,' said Tilly. They came to a stop, halfway down the hallway.

'Don't you want to see your boyfriend?' said Sally.

'I think she does,' said Tilly, nudging into Julia so that she was pushed against a door, which knocked against its frame. Julia felt the door give way behind her, so that where its solidity had pressed against her back, there was suddenly space into which she fell.

The tall man stood in the open doorway, looking down at her. Tilly and Sally had already run and Julia was alone with him. 'Come in,' he said, but Julia could not move. 'Come in,' he said again, reaching for her, and finally she stood on her weakened legs and stumbled away, towards the stairs and down, down to the entrance, the exit, holding onto the handrail all the way.

When Tilly moved to another town, Julia and Sally continued walking to and from school together, but they felt Tilly's absence. The two of them didn't see much of each other during the day. They still hung out after school sometimes but it wasn't the same. Sally mostly talked about other friends, and boys, one of whom lived in the tower block. She wanted Julia to come and hang out in the lobby with her, for the chance of encountering this boy, or even – having learnt which flat was his – to go and see where he lived.

Julia said all the flats looked the same from the outside, and anyway, she didn't want to go in there, to be anywhere near that place. Sally kept at her though, until she gave in.

As they entered the lobby, Julia half hoped the lift would be broken, and that Sally would not want to walk up to the boy's top-floor flat, but the lift was working just fine. They rode up. They had never been all the way up to the top, but it looked just the same as every other floor.

'What now?' asked Julia. 'Are you going to knock for him?'

'You do it,' said Sally.

'I don't know him,' said Julia.

'Just knock,' said Sally.

Julia moved tentatively towards the door and knocked, too quietly for Sally's liking, but as soon as she had done so – and heard movement from inside the flat – Julia felt certain that when the door opened the tall man would be there, that somehow she could knock on any one of these doors, any door on any floor in the entire building, and he would be there, inviting her in.

A lock or bolt was being undone. Julia turned and ran back down the hallway, back down the stairs, down flight after flight, until she could no longer hear the voice calling after her.

When she woke in the night, she saw, through a gap in the curtains, the tower block facing her. There was always a light on somewhere; it was a building that never quite slept.

She closed the gap, but the tower block got into her dreams. In the morning, she left the curtains closed.

She avoided the back of the house now. She spent as little time as possible in the kitchen, or else closed the blinds so she would not feel watched. Her mum let her eat her meals in the living room, in front of the TV. She came and went through the front door.

When she was outside, it was hard not to see the tower block, its grim hulk dominating the skyline, but she tried.

She thought she saw him once, in the corner shop. She walked out empty-handed, but by the time she got home she was no longer sure it had been him at all.

She got average grades at school and went to university through clearing. She struggled with her studies, and wondered if she had chosen the right course, if she had made a mistake, but she pressed on.

Her halls of residence had a payphone at the top of the stairs, from which she called her mum. There was still talk, said her mum, of the tower block being brought down. They made it sound like defeating a giant. It was still there when Julia visited, but apparently there was no one living in it now. The tower block really was going to be demolished. It was hard to imagine; they'd been living in its shadow for so long.

It was during Julia's particularly difficult final year that her mum died, and Julia moved home without completing her course. The tower block had gone, and she thought about the tall man, wondering if he had died or gone elsewhere. She was half expecting to see some remains, like the stump left behind when a tree was felled, but it was gone entirely, the plot freshly tarmacked and turned into parking. She would have expected there to be some celebration, but no one had much to say about it, only that it had been an eyesore and that it was high time.

People spoke gently about her loss, and neighbours brought round meals, casseroles, leaving them on the doorstep if Julia did not answer the door. They said of her mum, *She's with your dad now*, though he was spread far and wide. They had scattered his ashes in three different places, and Julia had worried about him feeling pulled apart, that what remained of him might want to be together, to be whole.

She had her mum's ashes interred at the cemetery. A plaque showed exactly where they were.

The house and everything in it had been left to Julia, who moved back into her childhood home, which felt vaguely strange. It looked just as it always had, except her bedroom had been turned into a guest room. And of course, the view was different now. She could eat a bowl of cereal at the kitchen table, and with the tower block gone, the light could get in; there was no shadow inching, every evening, towards the house.

Her mum had kept the place immaculate, so there was nothing for Julia to do, and yet she was feeling dog-tired, run-down; she could feel the tingle of a cold sore coming on. She wanted honey and lemon tea, but there was no honey in the cupboard so she made do with hot lemon squash. It wasn't quite bedtime, but she went to bed anyway. A good night's sleep would help, she thought. She had no cold symptoms, no headache or stomach ache or anything she could quite define, just a general, persistent malaise. When she heard knocking, she ignored it; often, it was just kids. Or perhaps it was the wind, she thought, when she stirred in the small hours, hearing the gentle rattling of a door in its frame.

She slept on and off until the middle of the afternoon, when she made her way down to the kitchen for more hot lemon squash, and some cereal if she could manage it. There was that knocking again, quiet but insistent at the back door. She opened up to see who it was but there was no one in sight. She stood there, in the still, heavy air, with the sunlight on her face.

There was something on the doorstep: not a casserole dish but a biscuit tin, and she thought something sweet would be nice. She picked it up and brought it inside. As she put it down on the kitchen counter, it occurred to her that it was just like the biscuit tin that the tall man had kept on his coffee table, but she didn't want to think about him any more. She thought about homemade cookies and lifted the lid, and found inside the biscuit tin that same old hair, the same tissue-wrapped packages, the same jumble of teeth. She half expected to see his missing fingers in there, as if this were a place in which to keep whatever had been lost, and then she touched a tissue-wrapped package and felt slender bones.

There was a label stuck to the side of the tin, bearing what she assumed to be his name: *The late Mr Harris*. She had always found that a strange term: 'your late father', and now 'the late Mr Harris', as if he had been delayed, as if were just caught in traffic and might arrive soon; and there was her own address, as if these remnants had been assigned to her, allotted to her. She imagined biscuit tins appearing on every doorstep in the terrace; grim reminders of the residents of that looming tower block.

But what was she expected to do with it? She didn't want it in the house. She could bin it: if she put it in the wheelie bin, the men would come and take it away. It would be sent to landfill, or burnt. But it didn't seem right to do that. Nor did she imagine Mr Harris approving of her treating so brutally these things that were, he had told her, more than keepsakes; they were talismanic.

She had left the back door wide open. A long shadow was reaching across the kitchen floor, as if a tall figure were standing in the doorway, though she could see there was nobody there. Now the shadow moved into the kitchen, and Julia backed against the counter, feeling the biscuit tin at her back. She watched as the door slowly closed, shutting out the sunlight until the shadow disappeared.

The Hermit

Steven J Dines

After Hayley left, taking Nick with her, the house seemed too big for just one person. Hayley took one hastily-filled suitcase and jumped into a taxi. When the van laughed up the next morning – driven by Martin, her good friend from work – and they took the rest of her stuff and all of Nick's clothes, furniture, and toys, the place suddenly felt huge, like some empty stadium at the end of days. For the last three months every one of their fights had ended on the same discordant note: *I need some space, Jeff.* But it seemed to Jeff Strange she was leaving a lot of that behind in order to move into some studio flat with her good friend from work.

What they did not take that Saturday morning, he bagged up on Sunday after skipping breakfast, which Hayl usually made for them both anyway. The best bacon rolls in London. She'd left him with limp shredded wheats and out-of-date semi-skimmed. He left the milk in the fridge door. Couldn't bring himself to pour it down the sink. To push its clots down the plughole.

Later, he found some of Hayley's clothes mixed in with his in the laundry basket. A couple of pink vest tops, a skirt, a pair of grey joggers left inside-out with her maroon knickers still twisted in there some quick change he had failed to notice at the time. In brutal silence, he separated everything out, hers from his, bagging her lot and then crying for fifteen minutes on the bathroom floor.

As difficult as that was, Nick's bedroom was worse. It was like walking into an abandoned theme park, some eerie, haunted place that still echoed with the ghost of his laughter. They took everything. Nick's Nerf guns. His Playmobil Ghostbusters collection, including the Marshmallow Man, Ecto 1, and those green splashes of ectoplasm he was always warning Nick not to put in his mouth. Gone. They took his posters, and even the Blu Tack *for* the posters. All they'd left behind were sweat stains on the walls from the missing Blu Tack and, abandoned in the middle of the floor, a Marvel Super Hero Masher with its left leg missing. Christ. They were thorough and they were fast. A cynical man would have said it had all been planned. Methodically. For months. Who on Earth took Blu Tack and Nerf bullets if they ever intended to return, Jeff wondered. His life had gone Chernobyl.

He scooped and bagged the amputee Spider-Man. He went to bed.

It was 11.00pm.

Standing at an upstairs window on Sunday evening, beer bottle in hand, he could see it all. The grass in the back garden needed a cut. Weeds threatening to take over like a virus. There were bald patches he hadn't noticed before on the lawn. As for the fence, it was crying out for weather seal. And while none of it ever truly bothered him before the separation (This isn't a break-up, he thought. No, nothing is broken here except…okay…*everything*), it made his skin itch with a special urgency now.

Isn't this supposed to happen in the weeks and months *after* the break-up? Follow the script, Jeff. Let the house go to rot and ruin and you along with it. One thing interchangeable with the other, especially since he would be spending most of his time here from now on, except maybe to skulk to the shops – the local one, not the busy supermarket – and then only for essentials like alcohol and bread. And there was his job too, he supposed. His fucking job. Those fucking people. He sighed at the mountainous, unscaleable prospect of it all. The very idea of rejoining society felt like a heavy, pressing bowel. He *could* cut the grass. Kill some weeds. Scatter some seed. Even seal the fence. But it would be like jumping the shark: some pathetic attempt to gain what, relevance? Respectability? He had been *cancelled*. Unceremoniously axed with no final episode to their seven seasons together. No satisfying conclusion. Nothing. They'd killed him off with some weak left-field plot twist by the name of Martin. Good friend from work Martin.

So let the fucking weeds grow.

He swiped his phone and hovered his thumb over 'Hayley' on his contacts list.

He drank from the bottle of beer. Lukewarm. The taste of failure.

He pressed 'Edit'. Replaced 'Hayley' with 'cold bitch'. All lower case.

He deleted the words. Retyped 'Hayley'.

Whatever she was, they had a son together. *He* had a son. Right? Or had the spin-off been pulled from him too?

The phone, the room, the garden of patches and weeds, it all swam in hot, sudden tears. The television show analogy wasn't working. There was no distance from this thing. Not yet. Not ever. Pain crushed his chest, trying to break through the cage around his heart. He downed the rest of the warm beer through a grimace.

Then Jeff Strange went online and ordered his first knife.

Monday, he rang the office and told his team leader he was ill. He'd need the week, he said.

On Wednesday, a female DPD van driver, red polo shirt, shorts, knocked on his door and handed him a cardboard box. Hers was the first real face he had seen since Hayley left on Saturday in a different van with Martin behind the wheel. Good friend from work – fuck it, he was growing to hate that song.

"Thank you thank you thank you," he said as he scratched out something that approximated his signature on the proof-of-delivery box. The woman seemed slightly bemused by his gratitude, and then like most people when he gave a little something of himself, she walked away.

He closed the door. Tried not to think about the driver. She was, like everything else right now, a mere ripple from the trussed-up body of their marriage Hayley had so enthusiastically dumped in the lake. Besides, the box in his hand was what was important to him right now. For the first time in days, his feet did not drag as he carried the box through to the kitchen and placed it on the island.

Nothing too fancy. A 20-centimetre chef's knife. Non-serrated blade. High carbon steel. Stone ground on both sides for a superior cutting edge. Carbonised ash wood handle.

Twenty-five-year guarantee. Which meant it stood a good chance of outlasting thirty-five per cent of all marriages. He'd Googled that little fact before he ordered the knife.

It cut, chopped, sliced, diced.

In other words: multi-purpose.

He held it up to the light reaching in through the blinds. Regarded his stubbled reflection in its blade, grateful he could not see his entire face at any one time. He looked different. Like someone else. Not Jeff.

Jeff was a piece of soft shit.

Still Wednesday.

Jeff took a shower. His first in days.

Something about the water though. It did not feel right on his skin. His skin did not feel right on his bones. His bones did not feel as though they belonged to him any more. Like his basic infrastructure was different now, broken now.

He looked for his small shaving mirror and found it gone, a pale sun on the tile where it used to be suckered to the wall. He could not believe Hayley would take it, but she had hated that he shaved in the shower so… Yes, she took it.

Jeff ran his hand along his rough jawline, tried to ignore how he had just referred to Hayley in the past tense, remembered the knife. Naked, he dripped downstairs and found it in the kitchen, still on the island but not quite how he had left it. Or how he *remembered* he had left it. He thought it would be lying out on the island, on its side, but instead the knife stood in the old walnut chopping block (Hayl had never liked that thing either because, she'd said, it was soft and cracked and unhygienic), stood like some long surfboard in a patch of dark sand. It was disorienting but also quite beautiful in a strange way.

Tears welled in his eyes then. Those words…one of their *things*. All marriages had them; all *good* marriages. In-jokes. As private, as intimate as any kiss; maybe more so. Once upon a time, in a place far far away it seemed, they would dress in their best clothes and go out for dinner together. "How do I look?" he'd ask Hayley. "Quite handsome," she'd say with that smirk of hers that melted his reactor core every time, "in a Strange way."

A cheap, easy pun. Priceless now.

He pulled the knife out of the chopping block where he had not left it. Looked at his pale reflection in the widest part of the blade, the heel.

He watched as Not Jeff tilted his stubbled cheek, fingered through his uncombed hair. Hayley could keep the shaving mirror, he decided. He had all he needed right here. Multi-purpose, all right.

He started to walk away from the island, from the kitchen, to head back to the still-running shower hissing emptily upstairs, when something happened in the heel of the knife.

The light from the kitchen window vanished, replaced by darkness. Deep and new and sudden, it seemed to shift from what looked like dark smoke rising from an unseen fire. Jeff – himself again; alone again – even felt his breath leave his throat as though stolen by a tremendous heat. But the shifting dark wasn't smoke, he realised. At least, not as he understood it. Smoke moved around your fingers, you couldn't really touch it. Smoke filled your mouth with its taste, your nose with its smell, your eyes with its pain. Jeff's eyes began to water now, looking into the knife, as though the smoke could reach his eyes. Tears slid down his face. In the darkness of the knife, he heard someone choking. Fingers sprang open, releasing the handle, dropping the knife. Instinctively, he checked himself for burns. As he heard the knife clatter on the vinyl floor tiles, he felt not heat but the chill of fear goosefleshing his arms.

As the initial shock began to wear off, Jeff's breathing grew desperate. He held his throat with both hands, cradling it almost, as though guiding it back to breath. The idea of another self seemed pathetic now, foolish, as his body refused to cooperate.

Breathe, he told this stranger who seemed suddenly in control of his most basic function. Just breathe.

Again and again. Until he pleaded: *Please...*

The stranger finally relented , but not until Jeff lay passed out on the kitchen floor.

Still Wednesday.

Jeff woke on the kitchen floor, a drool-puddle under his cheek. Upstairs, the shower was still running, the water long cold.

Climbing to his feet, he estimated he had been out for at least twenty minutes but no longer than an hour. He picked up the chef's knife from the floor, put it back on the island (*not* in the chopping block). From the corner of his eye he saw no darkness, no smoke, nothing else inside the blade. All of it, everything, seemed like a dream. Something far-off and foolish and ultimately pointless in retrospect. He hadn't been eating enough, drinking enough, *living* enough.

He hadn't been himself.

He took the cold shower that had been waiting impatiently for him but decided to give shaving a miss. Partway through, he realised he had showered earlier, before passing out. It all came back to him. He had stepped out for a moment to fetch the chef's knife from the kitchen and bring it upstairs to use as a shaving mirror, since Hayley had taken his. He stood in this second shower, inches outside its icy stream, and felt like a fucking idiot.

A fucking loser.

And then it struck him.

When did good friend from work Martin get so involved in Hayley's personal life? I thought he had a boyfriend. Hayley told me that. Wait – Hayley *told me that.*

A fucking idiot.

A fucking loser.

Jeff ordered the paring knife because the green apples in the bowl were becoming brown apples for the bin. He even paid extra for next-day delivery, but it arrived late, sometime on Friday, by which time the apples were too far gone. When the DPD van finally dragged up outside his house, with the same female driver that had delivered the chef's knife behind the wheel, Jeff was livid but tried his best to contain it to mild irritation. Nevertheless, the front door was open before she made it halfway up the path.

"You're late."

Startled, she glanced at her wrist. She wore one of those smartwatches that count the number of steps the wearer takes. Hayley had bought him one but the numbers were only a daily reminder he was going nowhere.

"It was supposed to be delivered yesterday," he said.

"I'm here now," she replied, emerging on the other side of Jeff's ambush with a professional smile perfectly mustered. "If you can just sign here, please."

She offered Jeff the device and pen.

"What's your name?" he asked.

"Audrey," she said. "Sign here, on the screen. Thanks."

Her name evoked a younger woman, black hair, Fifties look, swaying in a fitted sweater and plaid wool skirt to some slow, hypnotic jazz. A woman who could tie a knot in a cherry stalk with her tongue. *This* woman wore a red polo shirt, shorts, was touching forty-five, brown roots overrunning bottle-blonde, and if she was swaying it wasn't to Angelo Badalamenti but to the music of a urinal somewhere in her near future.

"You don't look like an Audrey," he said.

He saw her wonder how to take it, then decide how she would.

"You don't look like a Richard either, but…"

"My name isn't… Ah. Got you. Let me…let me just sign for this and you can get on your way."

"That would be great, sir. Thank you."

Jeff wrote *R. Sorry* on the screen. First name Really. She didn't look at what he wrote. Maybe she would notice later. She handed over the parcel and headed back to her van, to the next difficult customer. He really was sorry. And now he was also annoyed for missing every cue in his life. The one for being polite. The one for confronting his wife about fucking someone else. Every cue in between.

Jeff stood at the front door and watched Audrey walk away. Back to her van, back to her life. With her blonde ponytail wagging, she seemed like some cheerful toy dog let off its leash to run a field. And with that, Jeff realised, his charm needed a lot of work. A *lot*.

She coaxed a little smile out of him though.

Richard, he thought. As in…

"Good one, Audrey."

He went inside.

In the kitchen, he stood at the island and moved the surfboard in the sand – the chef's knife standing in the chopping block again – to make some room before he tore into the parcel.

Polypropylene handle. Twin rivets. Chromium-molybdenum-vanadium steel.

A 2.75-inch bird's beak blade. As beautiful as its own alliteration.

Like the chef's knife, it was too good for drawer space. It had a place and a presence in this room, in this house. It made itself known. Besides, he no longer had Nick around to worry about. He could leave every knife and sharp object in the house lying out if he wanted to. He could turn the place into a *house* of knives... And wouldn't *that* take him as far away as possible from this house and all its memories?

I wonder how he's coping? Better than me? Better than this? God, I hope so.

Jeff gripped the paring knife in his left hand. It wasn't as bold as the chef's; all handle with a short, curved blade. You could leave the chef lying out and it made a statement on its own, but the paring...it needed propping up, just a little help to shine. He decided it should stand, leaning, inside a mug on the kitchen island. Hayley had taken the tree and most of the mugs along with it, but she'd left him a couple of his own. Birthday or Father's Day presents from Nick. She'd taken their son and left him those.

He stood back to assess how the paring knife fit into its new home. With that short, curved blade it looked like a hungry bird in a ceramic nest. Beak raised, waiting for the return of its parents.

Hayley did not accept his first call and let the second ring for too long. Jeff's finger was poised to hang up when her voice pushed out of the phone's speaker.

"Hello."

"It's Jeff."

"I know. What do you want?"

"How's Nick?"

"Nick's...fine. I think this feels like some big adventure to him."

That's one.

"He might just be putting on a brave face," he said.

"Maybe. Seven-year-olds tend to go with the flow though."

That's two.

"Has he been asking questions?"

"Of course. He's curious."

"And?"

"And what, Jeff?"

"What has he been asking?"

"Just the kind of things you'd expect. If Daddy is okay. If he's coming to visit."

"*Can* I see him?"

"You don't have to ask – well, for the sake of practical arrangements, yes, but I'm not being difficult, Jeff. He's still your son and you're still his father, even if you and I are not – you know – the same."

"I miss him. I miss you both. I love you both."

"He loves you too. But you scared him. You scared *us*. You need some time. Speak to someone and get…get the help you need. Nick will still be here. He can't stop being your son. It isn't that simple. Or that easy."

Three.

"But he's okay though?"

"Yes, he's okay."

"Good. Good."

"Look, Jeff, I need to go—"

"I am, you know. Speaking to someone…"

"Really, that's…that's good news. I hope it works out."

"Her name is Audrey. She comes to the house. We talk."

"Audrey? Okay. Well, I hope Audrey can help you work through some things. I'm sorry, Jeff, but I have to go. Call me in a couple of days. We can arrange for you to see Nick. He still wants to play crazy golf with you."

"I won't do that."

"Okay, Jeff. Whatever. We'll arrange *something*."

"She brings me knives."

"What? Who does?"

"Audrey. She brings them to me. To my door."

Jeff listened to Hayley's loud breathing on the speaker while he waited for her to say something.

"Why would someone do that, Jeff?"

"I buy them. She brings them to the house. It's my new hobby, I think."

"You think? Are you…are you trying to *frighten* me?"

"No. No, not at all."

"Stop talking like that then."

"Was he ever gay? Martin? Your good friend from work Martin."

"No, Jeff. Martin wasn't gay."

Four.

"And you're living with him now, aren't you?"

"Yes, I am."

"So you lied to me."

"Yes. I'm sorry."

"You lied so I would let my guard down. So I'd let you two spend time together."

"This conversation didn't take long."

"So I'd invite him into my fucking house, Hayley. My fucking *home*."

Five and six and seven and…

"Jeff? Jeff? Listen to me. I'm sorry but I am not doing this, not anymore. It's over. I can't. Look, maybe you should stay away from Nick for a while. It's not what I want, not really, but the way you're acting… *talking*… It doesn't seem like a good idea."

"How do you *expect* me to act, Hayley? I've lost you. I've lost everything."

"I lost you too," she said. "Years ago. I begged you, Jeff. I *pleaded* with you to come back to me – to get some help. The doctors *can* help you, if you let them in. But you – you and your fucking male pride… Look, I—I can't. I just can't. Don't call me for a while. Text me when you're better. Then you can see Nick."

Call ended.

Jeff looked down at his hands, at the single smear of blood on the tip of his index finger, at the chef's knife lying on the kitchen island, handle clean but the blade bloodied from the point to the belly. He could not remember pulling it from the chopping block or it entering his side. Six, seven, maybe eight shallow cuts, bleeding. Like a whore, he had not felt the penetration. Like a virgin, he panicked when he saw the blood. He grabbed a dish towel and pressed it to the wounds. Watched it turn red and red and red.

I didn't do this, he thought. I *didn't*.

Eventually the bleeding stopped, but the hurt and confusion remained. Upstairs, he layered hour-glass-shaped plasters across his side as his laptop took forever to power up.

I lost you too, Hayley had said. *I pleaded with you to come back to me.*

Where did I go? Jeff wondered.

Where was he now?

The laptop booted, he opened a browser.

Ordered more knives.

Saturday was the hottest day of the year. Jeff got up at midday and sat on the sofa in his boxer shorts in the living room with the curtains drawn, watching television while the world burned. He hoped Hayley remembered to put suntan lotion on Nick. Not Factor 20 either but SPF 30, to be safe. The boy's arms were like kindling and just as likely to burn.

On the BBC News, they were reporting another stabbing in Hackney. A seventeen-year-old male was in critical condition. The suspect, another male, sixteen, was still on the run. These boys – and they were usually that, *boys* – giving the capital a bad name. Giving knives a bad name. The newsreaders kept repeating the sound bite *knife crime*, but the problem wasn't the knives. Take the knives out of their hands and those boys would find other ways to hurt each other and themselves.

Jeff changed the channel. Watching the news meant letting the world in. But the other channels weren't any better. Every film contained a kissing scene, every game show a wife with a husband and child back home, every talent show an orchestrated story of loss or struggle to tug tug tug at the heart strings. Shopping channels sold cheap gift sets, *ideal for the man or woman in* your *life*, while children's channels reminded him of watching cartoons with Nick on a Saturday morning, only now every presenter seemed like a predator who had stolen his son away, groomed him for a life apart from his father. They distributed their own special brand of cheer too, these pushers of so-called happiness, presenting to the impressionable young only one side of the moon, its happy, sunlit, smiling face. The dark side they left for the adults and Pink Floyd to contemplate.

He changed the channel and changed the channel without ever really changing the channel at all.

Jeff turned off the television. In the plunging silence, with the curtains drawn and only just holding back the world trying to push in from the other side, the house stirred with memories.

He sat there and stared at the open-legged middle-aged middleweight reflected in the darkness of the screen. His distended belly. His receding hair. His hidden crotch. All of it captured in a moment of abject vulnerability: a man. Jeff Strange. Strange Jeff.

Hayley did not understand. He did not *want* her to understand. It was his weakness. His failure. His coming up short. Some men did not want to grow up. But some men simply could not. They were stuck in a time; worse, in a mindset. You don't mature beyond the moment you began to hate yourself.

He was twelve years old when he first wanted to die. He would be twelve forever. They call it the black dog. They even try to soften it by making some tenuous association with man's best friend. It isn't a dog. It isn't *just* black. It's a parasite and its colour is the vacuum of deep outer space that exists apart from anything like stars.

He stood from the sofa and the space around *him* flexed with memories. They moved around him like moons tied to his gravitational pull, cold, untouchable rocks controlling the tide of his mood even as he urged them away, away. He glanced back at the sofa he had risen from. The cushion was forgetting him even as he watched, slowly reshaping itself as though he had never been there at all. How many times had they sat here together holding hands? How many films had they watched while spooning, until the pressing of Hayley against him had overwhelmed the plot and led to them making love? Nick was conceived right here, he thought. A quickie one day after work. Hayley had been waiting for him at the bottom of the stairs, naked. As soon as he had walked in the front door, she pounced: a light kiss on the cheek then leading him literally by the crotch into the living room. No time to go upstairs, she'd said. It had to be *now*. It had been hot in the sense that dry gears grinding against each other generated heat; friction and discomfort and moments when he had thought he could not ejaculate. But thanks to her ovulation calculator, Hayley had turned him into a performing animal in the circus of conception, throwing him a treat then expecting feats of poise and skill, like some knife-throwing bear balanced on a board and cylinder while trying to hit a target blindfolded. The image and the memory of it now made him smile, and then laugh, and then cry.

Wiping his eyes, he left the room. The floating planets of memory plummeted to the floor, through it, as the room awaited his return, seeming to listen to his footsteps crossing the kitchen tile, there and back, until Jeff returned with the chef's knife in his hand.

He plunged it into the sofa arm. He heard no sound inside the living room except his own loud grunt of effort. No ripping, splitting, screaming. It led him to a moment of contemplation and regret. Had it made him feel better?

What was the point of this? No, and no point, but it had to be done. It had to be *now*. So, he withdrew the knife and plunged it right back in again, the same hole, deeper this time, the knife's blade chiming against some part of the framework or perhaps a bolt or screw.

And then you went ahead and lost it for a while, removed from yourself, stabbing and slashing and twisting and stabbing until the sofa's skin lay in strips across the room and you were ankle-deep in a field of polyfibre snow.

Standing there, aching, gasping, you watched as those other memories rose from the floor around you once more, resuming their old orbits until, tired of killing the sofa, you turned and gave them your full attention. You studied their paths until just the right moment, and then threw the ten-inch chef's knife at one of them – the afternoon less than two months ago when Jeff returned home from the office to find Hayley and Martin sitting on the sofa, talking not fucking but still flushed of face. She had introduced him as a friend, turning the sofa into a liar and a co-conspirator, and if not those then a *supporter* of lies – and the knife shuddered as it lodged itself in the wall, the thing impaled on the cracked plasterboard not a planet any more but a monstrous insect of memory, body pinned, legs, wings, twitching.

You ran from the room and thundered up the stairs where you showered for over an hour and then dressed in two. While you were gone, soaping the guilt from your dirty skin, you thought you heard the living room stop holding its breath and begin to quietly sob.

Déjà vu.

A walk in a park.

Jeff did not know which park it was. It didn't matter. He rarely looked up from his feet sliding in and out of his field of vision. London and the rest of the world existed outside of that. Went on without him.

He had been walking for hours though. He could be anywhere. Anywhere he could reasonably reach by foot and travelling at two or three miles per hour. So, not very far at all.

Wherever he was, he had fresh air. The house was getting stuffy and stale. It dawned on him he could open a window, let in some air. It dawned on him miles away from any of the fucking windows.

Twat.

It was Saturday. Afternoon. Or was it Sunday? Did he really have to go back to work tomorrow? He picked up the pace a little, hoping to outdistance Monday, but he only grew tired and Monday only drew closer. He realised it was in fact Saturday anyway, and just like that Sunday was given back to him. The knife he had ordered wouldn't arrive until Monday though, and what if he was at work when she, no, the knife, arrived at the house? He'd find a card that read *sorry we missed you!* and have no parcel to open. Getting through Monday really seemed like a roll of the dice.

There were other people here too, he noticed. He moved among them in his black hoodie like a ghost. They were mostly walking around or sunbathing on the grass. Couples Snapchatting their lovers on their phones. Singles reading paperbacks or Kindles. Others simply closing their eyes and praying to the god of skin cancer. Every last one of them lost in their fictions.

Jeff wondered what Hayley and Martin were doing. On a day like this, he would probably take them out for a drive somewhere in his big fancy SUV. Jeff could see them stopping off somewhere for ice cream. He hoped Nick ordered chocolate or blue raspberry or anything brightly coloured, and he hoped it was hot inside Martin's car and Nick's ice cream melted onto the back seat. He hoped Martin got mad at Nick and Hayley saw him for what he truly was: a control freak or someone who valued things over people or a man who did not know how to talk to children that weren't his.

But Jeff could recall the times he'd met Martin and some of the nice things Hayley had said about him when Jeff believed they were just good friends, and he had seemed like a decent bloke. One of the good guys.

Which is why the sofa is dead, he thought.

The truth was: if Nick *did* drip ice cream onto Martin's seats, he imagined Martin would give Nick a reassuring smile in the rear-view mirror and hand the boy some napkins. Saying, *It's okay son.*

Then Martin's eyes shifted in the rear-view mirror, focused on Jeff, who until that instant hadn't realised he was part of this scene playing out in his mind.

It's Hackney Downs, Martin said in the mirror and in Jeff's ear. *That's where you are. And I brought you here so maybe you'd meet the nice lad with the knife. Problem solved, Strange Jeff. Problem solved.*

Jeff stumbled. Recovering, he shook his head as if to somehow loosen the grip of the thought and the voice on his mind. Wherever he was—

Is it Hackney Downs? Yes, it is.

—he suddenly wanted to be home. He wanted Hayley to be there. And Nick too, playing in his room. They could even look for Spider-Man's missing leg together.

He had a panic attack then as the real world rushed into his lungs and all the air rushed out. It was twenty-six degrees in the capital and he found himself falling back against the trunk of a London Plane in Hackney Downs, sweating, dizzy, tearing the hoodie off himself as he fought to breathe and as what felt like a knife stabbed him in the chest over and over again.

Jeff waited for the attack to either subside or kill him.

It subsided.

He leaned against the trunk, looked up at the patterns of the leaves, like a green cloth threatening to smother him, and thought, Today is the bottom. It has to be. It can't get any worse than this.

He had to do more. Get more. Take back control.

On the way back home, he stopped at a supermarket and deep-breathed and head-downed his way directly to the kitchenware aisle. He did not pass Go. He did not collect £200.

What he did get was a boning knife and a six-inch cleaver.

Less than a mile from the office, stuck in early morning London traffic in his Fiesta, listening to the Eagles sing *Desperado*, raining but no rainbow in sight, Jeff knew he was not going to be his old self at work today. Monday mornings were always bad but he did not know what he was going to walk into, awkward silences or a barrage of awkward questions. Either way: awkward. Hayley had already updated her relationship status on Facebook, which he only discovered that morning dressing for work, and it fucking hurt, like some public declaration of his failure. He couldn't get the Windsor knot tight enough.

Driving into the multistorey car park felt like arriving at his own crypt. He hesitated turning the key to kill the engine. He thought about driving away. But driving where? Feeling the early clutchings of another panic attack, he parked, released the seat belt, opened the window, and breathed deep the stale air. The muscles around his lungs squeezed like fists around two squirming grey mice.

Jeff reached across to open the glovebox, and a bunch of Hayley's compilation CDs clattered into the passenger footwell along with something else. Hayley had always been one for greatest hits and Best Ofs. Musically, Jeff had liked to wander off the beaten path a little more to find those underappreciated album tracks no one else seemed to visit. But he wasn't looking for music. It was the something else he wanted.

You lifted the boning knife from the footwell and let it rest on your lap without letting go of the oversized twin-rivet handle. Oversized to maximise grip while working in slippery butchering environments.

You closed your eyes and traced the length of the spine between the tip of your index finger and thumb. Smooth, like Braille for a lonely man. And if you could not read the imperfections in its silence, then maybe its imperfections – and yours – simply did not exist. You centred in that thought, and felt the fingers around those little grey mice inside your chest extend and release... *And breathe.*

Reluctantly, Jeff returned the knife to the glovebox and closed the lid. He left the CDs scattered on the floor as a deterrent to anyone who might consider stealing the car. A deterrent besides the car itself, which did not scream out *steal me* in the first place. If there was one thing he would not miss it was turning on the engine some mornings to Westlife kicking his ear drums in. He'd love to throw those lads over a cliff sometime, yelling after them, "Try it without wings now, you cunts!"

He laughed as he got out of the car. A real belly laugh. He laughed until there were tears running down his cheeks. Until he staggered into the office foyer ten minutes later. Until the lift arrived. By the time he was flying (without wings) toward the ninth floor with Marcella from Accounts, Jeff was biting his lip and rubbing the wet salt from his eyes.

He felt Marcella's hand pat his back. *There there.*

They'd almost had a thing once, long ago, but the mildly flirtatious emails and the exchanged glances when they passed in the soft-carpeted corridors of Saunders and Townsend were just Marcella being friendly and then him being over-friendly and then nothing. Not that he would have ever cheated on Hayley but sometimes a man wanted someone to throw a little oxygen at the shrinking flames of his ego.

Marcella's hand had not left his back, but she wasn't patting him any more. She was rubbing concentric circles over his left shoulder blade. Massaging his broken heart. He realised Marcella thought his Westlife tears were real.

Bad timing *again*, Jeff thought.

"I heard about what happened with your wife," she said. Soothing voice. "If you ever need to talk, you know where I am."

But Jeff's mind had already drifted somewhere else. Drifted to the parcel he was expecting to be delivered later today. Drifted toward thoughts like, would he make it home in time? Would there be one of those cards, crumpled like a dead flower, behind his door? Or would fate arrange it so he pulled up outside the house at the same time the parcel of steak knives arrived? And would the delivery driver be Audrey?

Six sets of six steak knives came to thirty-six knives in total. One for every year of his life, he realised. He had to respect the neatness of that: the patterns that were somehow thrown his way, seemingly random and yet perhaps not; perhaps suggestive of some hidden force at play, natural, supernatural, good, evil, whatever, but with an agenda all of its own.

Of course, maybe he was just seeing something that wasn't really there. Like Hayley and Martin as friends. Like meanings in emails. Like Westlife broken on a phalanx of rocks.

Connections that did not and never did exist.

The lift arrived on nine and Jeff walked over to his desk feeling deflated from each rising floor. It was fifteen minutes before he realised he had left Marcella standing there in the lift, having walked away from her without saying a word. By that point he had other things on his mind.

Like what it was he did around here.

And how, every time he clicked his pen, he thought of a flick knife.

Still Monday.

Work survived. No card left behind the front door.

Jeff paced the house, although it felt like the house was pacing him: he felt the footfall of its memories as he went from one near-empty room to the next. It was stalking him, he realised. Like one of those young lads walking home through these darkened London streets, not knowing that for no logical reason at all they would be stuck tonight, killed tonight. He gripped the contoured handle of the cleaver as he swung it at his side. Triple rivet. Anti-slip. He felt safe in its hands. Occasionally, he swung the cleaver down diagonally in front of him, two o'clock to seven, ten o'clock to five, just to hear it parting the air, a whistle as it worked, as it slashed at something hidden. Opened a seam that he could walk on through.

Doorbell. The first chime but not the second. Jeff waited for it, the second, but it never came and it never came, and into that lengthening silence he felt a dam inside him burst and floodwaters of anxiety rushing through all the valleys of his insides. He all but ran to the door, and all but forgot to return the cleaver to the kitchen before opening it.

"Parcel for you," she said. "Sign the screen, please."

"*Audrey*," he said in such a way that left him blushing. He wanted to immediately close the door and take an hour to straighten himself out. But what would one hour achieve that twenty years had not, he thought. "It's good to see you."

She took Jeff in.

"Rough day?" she asked.

His hand went to his unshaven face, an unconscious action that collapsed the whole house of cards as his shirt came fully untucked and he flashed a sweat-stained armpit. Even under the scrutiny of her kind brown eyes, Jeff felt suddenly self-conscious. It was like opening a door to find his house ransacked. He diverted his eyes away from hers. Down. To his mismatched socks.

Focusing instead on the cardboard box Audrey had laid at her feet, he took a breath and tried to explain. "My wife left."

"Oh… I'm…"

After a long day of co-workers reaching for the book of cliches, Jeff shook his head, "It's okay. Well, it's *not* but…it is what it is. I'm coping."

"Clearly," she said, then gave an embarrassed laugh. "Sorry, that came out wrong." She smirked but Jeff sensed it wasn't at him. If anything, she was standing on his doorstep inviting him in. "In fact, I'm *really sorry*. Just like you. You know…I get a lot of strange signatures in this job but trust me that was one of the nicest ones."

"Funny you should say that. My name is Strange."

"Well duh – I know that."

"Of course. Anyway, what you said? It's fine. Fair comment actually. I appreciate the honesty. It's been in short supply."

"Well, I've had my fair share of heartaches," she said. "And after so many your tolerance for bullshit becomes lowered somewhat. That and not being seventeen any more, I've outgrown the fairytale phase of my life."

"That's sad to hear."

"Is it?" Audrey shrugged. "I don't think so. Girls learn pretty early on the frog stays a frog no matter how much you kiss him or will him to change. Meanwhile, the handsome prince, he's just a narcissist who thinks it's okay to hit women."

Audrey smiled. Raised eyebrows, open face.

"Give me a humble peasant any day," she said. "But with a six-pack – *obviously*. Now, do you want to sign for this or would you like me to deconstruct Snow White for you?"

Jeff held up his hands in surrender. "I'll sign, I'll sign. You've ruined fairytales for me forever."

"Dangerous things," she said, passing the device. "Oh, the pen's somewhere in the van. Can you use your finger?"

Jeff blushed. Could not look her in the eye. He wrote on the device, a word he hoped Audrey would be able to read later on, feeling like a giddy child at the beach drawing patterns in the sand.

"Would you mind if I use the ladies?"

Audrey's question startled him. Before he could give it any thought, he stepped aside, pushing the door to open a path for her to the stairs.

"We're not supposed to do this," she said. "Against company policy. But I had an extra coffee this morning before shift and it was definitely one too many. You don't look like an angry prince with mummy or daddy issues, so...where am I going?"

"Up," he said. "Stairs," he said. "Third door on the right."

She entered the house. Red polo shirt, shorts. Before he stopped her partway up the stairs by saying her name, Jeff spotted something on the back of her neck. A tattoo. A zip slider, the closed teeth disappearing beneath the polo's neckline.

"So the whole 'Happily Ever After' thing," he said. "What's your take on that?"

"Oh, that's a big lie too," she replied, matter-of-factly. "Like the kiss that awakens the princess into the world of men. It's really the prince who's been asleep if he thinks one kiss will solve all her problems. Basically, it's men thinking with *that*, as usual. Third door on the right, right?"

Jeff nodded. He watched her climb the stairs.

You watched her climb.

Red polo shirt, shorts. You liked that her appearance never changed. You liked that she brought you knives. You closed the front door, even though Audrey was still inside the house, upstairs, lowering her shorts, sitting, peeing. There was no lock on the bathroom door; not any more. Anyone could walk in on her. You wondered if, when she realised there was no lock, she would have second thoughts about the lowering of her shorts and the peeing. But from the simple fact the house was quiet and she had not reappeared on the stairs, it was clear urgency had taken over, like it always did. And there she was, up there, potentially putting herself in harm's way to satisfy a basic need.

You felt the air inside the house change then, as though the walls themselves held onto a breath as you held onto yours. In the kitchen, a metallic rattling sound as every knife you had bought since Hayley left floated inches above the spot where it had lain moments before, handles pointed toward windows and walls, out, outward, rivets glaring from black handles like gimlet eyes, the tip of every blade pointing in, inward, into the house. Dozens of knives floated impossibly in the air, suspended in the silence of the breath caught in your throat. Knives, walls, house, you all listened to the faint sound of Audrey upstairs, urinating. And then you realised the knives were tracking the sound, pee making contact with toilet water, pointing like accusing fingers apportioning blame. You feared what might happen when she walked down those stairs again, bladder empty, how her smile would fade as she walked among the knives gathered, waiting, toward a door you are not sure the house would allow you to open. *No*, you thought. *It's not the house. It's you. It's your fault this happened. You're the one to blame.* Or would you turn to reach for the handle (door or knife handle, Jeff? *Strange* Jeff) to set her free, only to feel the tiny breaths of knives on the back of your neck as they hurtled themselves towards hers, towards that nexus of thin skin, thin flesh.

Jeff opened his eyes. He glanced into the kitchen and saw there were no knives floating in there, or anywhere else for that matter. They lay on their sides across the island, the scales of some larger thing, a great silver fish, he thought, catching the sun's light through the blinds.

He heard the sound of the toilet-flush followed rapidly by Audrey's footsteps on the bathroom floor, the landing, the stairs. It was obvious something *had* happened. Her face looked pale and she seemed unsteady on her feet, almost tripping down the last of the stairs on her way to the door. Audrey was now Not Audrey like he was sometimes Not Jeff. Scared, alone, trying to escape.

Why do people do that, he thought. Why does no one stay themselves for very long?

"Is everything okay?" he asked.

Audrey nodded but she was not okay. She was far from okay. She looked rattled, like she had seen a ghost. Or been touched by one.

"Open the door, please." Her voice, like her, trembling.

Jeff opened the door. There was no moment of resistance; no thought of it. The house did not seem to have a problem with Audrey leaving. It was only history repeating itself, after all. Different houses, maybe, but the leaving was the same. They all left; they all ran, leaving him alone with that other thing.

Whatever happened upstairs there was a rational explanation for it, just like there was for what happened down there with him and the floating knives. A moment of madness. A house needing to fill itself. Satiate its hunger. It wanted to be lived in, not haunted by the ghosts of its painful memories. But when even the good memories were painful, it all became…too much.

Audrey hurried down the path and practically leapt into her van and drove off. Jeff stood at the door and stood at the door. Minutes passed. Cool air brushed his burning face. Hot tears filled his eyes. The world became a blur. All its sharp edges smoothed. He wanted it to stay that way forever, a place where nothing had any real shape or form, like an unfinished painting.

Eventually, he went inside, drawn upstairs to the bathroom and the thing that had frightened Audrey so. He stood at the door without stepping inside. Strange as it sounded, it was a respect thing. The room was still warm with her presence and he thought he should give it – and her – time to cool off. The toilet seat was still down, the lid still up. Maybe Audrey had sat on the toilet, knees together, underwear around her shins, humming a tune to herself. Maybe she had flicked the end of the toilet roll for distraction. Maybe she had just looked around.

He saw it.

The shower curtain, which had been drawn all the way across, was halfway open. Audrey had opened it. Maybe she had watched the film *Psycho* when she was a child. Something like that left a lifelong impression if someone was exposed when they were too young, too innocent. Maybe Audrey was the type who could not leave the wardrobe open when she went to bed at night. He had not pegged her as being squeamish, not in the slightest. The zip tattoo on her neck, for instance. He'd seen them before on the internet. A scar tattoo. She'd had surgery at some point and the tattoo was to cover up something ugly with something good. To put herself back together again after an operation, maybe one when she was very young. That made sense, right? He realised he did not know her at all, and that sinking realisation made the word he had written on her handheld device for her to read later on seem foolish, dangerous even. *Drink?* Who would want to go for a drink with him after seeing what she had seen?

Fucking idiot.

Fucking loser.

The bath was full of knives.

The knives kept coming.

Some deliveries they left on Jeff's doorstep. Some they unceremoniously tossed over the back garden wall. Day after day, week after week, when Audrey never showed up, he went on the internet, sometimes into its dark corners, and ordered more knives. In those rare moments when he did attempt to find some clarity in his thinking, he wondered: was he buying them in the hope of seeing Audrey again, a woman he knew very little about, with whom he had shared a frisson of connection, or was it to fill some need in his psyche? Or, was it c), none of the above? He reasoned it this way: if he woke up every morning and found a deep hole dug into his lawn, should he not at least try to fill it, day after day after day? It was simply part of his routine, his life, like pulling on the same shirt for work or brushing his teeth with an empty brush. Filling holes. Buying knives.

For a while Jeff told himself he was getting them off the streets. He was healing the fucking world, man. But another three young Londoners had died recently because of his obsession, making it abundantly clear he wasn't saving anyone. But nothing should stop him trying. He began rationing food and leaving bills unpaid so he could afford to place one more order, buy one more knife.

He became good at it, too.

Finally, he thought. *Something.*

He went from fast food to Michelin star. Steak knives were fine for a quick, easy fix but they did not satisfy the hunger for very long. He also outgrew the larger chefs and carvers, preferring the more compact knives instead. Pocket knives became his new thing, where the focus was on the blade: straight backs and hawksbills, sheepsfoots and wharncliffes, clip points and drop points, points of all types, in fact; tanto, trailing, needle, spear. It was for practical reasons mostly; the kitchen island and countertops were overflowing. Besides, smaller knives meant *more* knives. But then, he also went bigger, so maybe there was a flaw somewhere in his thinking. The machetes were genuine works of knife art, beautiful, curving extensions of the arm, and when he swung them they did not whistle through the air but created a kind of music. Kukris and bolos. Pangas and tapangas, goloks and latin, heavy and cane. Knives, yes, but poetry for the soul. Each handle as unique as the blade it held, embraced, gave to the world, and while some welcomed the hand, others persuaded the hand to welcome it.

Every day, he carried one of the pocket knives with him into work. A stockman. With foldable blades and cutting edges of less than 7.62 centimetres, it was legal to carry. The billhook machete he stowed beneath the seat of his car less so. But Jeff decided it was worth the risk. Just having them around – or in the case of the stockman, in his pocket – meant he felt less vulnerable. More like a man. Yes, that. A man who could protect himself. Increasingly, he felt he was changing, hardening. He had knives in his blood; ice-tempered steel in his veins. He was Not Jeff.

One lunchtime at work, Marcella approached his desk. This act alone was newsworthy as he had noticed how other people around the office avoided him. Gazes fell to the carpeted floor in passing. Nods replaced actual conversation. He found himself dropped from coffee rounds. They were simply stepping around the body of the man he used to be, he decided, and he was fine with that.

"Hey. You wouldn't have a pen I could borrow, would you?" she asked.

Marcella. Jeff liked her. Petite, thin, built to move. She was a throwing knife.

"Of course," he said. He went to open his drawer but his hand paused. Inside, he realised, there was more than paper-clips and pens. "You know what? I actually don't have any spare."

Her eyebrows raised.

"I'm not joking," he said.

She smiled as though he was.

"Seriously. I don't have one. You'll need to ask someone else."

The smile faded and an awkward silence pushed between them. Marcella nodded slowly, gravely, really disappointed about the pen.

Jeff wiped sweat from his forehead and watched her walk back to her desk on the far side of the office. Past other desks. Past other pens.

Why did she come all the way over here to ask *me*? He thought.

Some days later, or maybe it was weeks, a knock on the door.

Jeff was in the bathroom, shaving with a pocket knife. Hayley was dropping off Nick so they could spend some father son time together, she'd said. He'd asked her politely not to call it that. *We're just going to hang out. I've missed him.* The knock at the door, a little earlier than the agreed time, startled Jeff, and his hand slipped. Just a little. But he stood there for a moment, reflected in a cleaver propped between the taps on the bathroom sink, bleeding into the foam, red blooming through the white.

A second knock brought him back. Jeff drew a small towel down his face, along his jaw, answered the door.

Delivery.

Not Audrey. A man.

The man handed over the device for signing but not before he waved his finger over his own jawline to let Jeff know he was still bleeding. Jeff took the pen, wrote his name and nothing more. The man handed him the parcel, nodded. Jeff closed the door on him.

He pressed his forehead to the cool glass of the two-lite door. He just knew something in his bones today: it was going to be a day of a thousand cuts; maybe even *the* day. The black dog was sat outside his house, pawing to get in. *Come* in then, he thought. I've got a handmade Damascus steel Bowie right here with your name on it.

But he dropped the parcel to the floor, unopened.

Through the door glass he saw the shape of someone else stood outside.

Jeff opened the door.

"Audrey!"

She looked different, and it took him a moment to realise she was out of the red polo shirt and shorts of her daily uniform and dressed like a real person. White long-sleeve top over a flared floral skirt, thong sandals. That, and her face was pulled into a rictus grin, off-putting for a moment, but Jeff wasted no time saying what he had wanted to say to her the day she fled and every day since.

"Let me explain the thing with the knives… Some people – some people buy books they don't ever read, right? They fill their houses with them. Those books, okay? They only turn into *stories* if you read them. Otherwise, they're just books. Objects. No meaning at all. I buy knives but I don't *use* them. Hayley leaving the way she did, taking my son, someone else being involved, I threw myself into it. Way way *way* into it. But they're nothing. Like books I've never opened. Stories I've never read. What I'm trying to tell you is I'm not dangerous, Audrey. I swear."

"So why do it? Why buy them, and buy so *many?*"

With a shrug, he said, "I don't know. I feel better with them around, I think. Protected. No, distracted. I don't know. Something. I'll be honest with you—"

"Please do."

"—I don't completely understand it."

"You and me both. It's Strange, Jeff."

"That's me. Strange Jeff."

"It's isn't funny. It's really fucking weird."

"I know, I know. And I *really* wanted to go for that drink with you. To find out if there was something there or not. You know, a spark. Something."

"Oh, there *is*," she said, and pulled him in for a kiss.

Something did not feel right. He thought it might be his lingering loyalty to Hayley that made Audrey's face pressed against his feel odd and cold, but it was *how* she kissed him, he realised. She kissed him still wearing that rictus grin. Like she was afraid to relax. To get into the moment. To open her mouth.

Jeff held her upper arms and eased her away, breaking the kiss.

"Is this really happening?"

"What do *you* think?"

"I don't know. I want it to be real but something's not right. You ran…"

"I did."

"You came back."

"I did that too."

"Something's not right," he said again but with less conviction. "Besides, my wife and son will be here soon. I'm spending the day with him. I haven't seen him since she left. I—"

Audrey pressed a fingertip to his lips. "You don't have to explain. *That* I do get. You want me to go – for now. You want me to come back later, say around eight, and bring a bottle of wine so we can have that drink you wanted. Sound good?"

"Sounds…unexpected," he said. "But good. Definitely good."

She leaned toward him and kissed him again, on the left cheek, the side of his face he'd cut while shaving with a pocket knife. He decided he wasn't going to tell her about that. For Audrey, he would go back to using a razor. But the kiss, again, felt peculiar, clenched teeth and closed-mouthed, teeth on cheekbone, hardness on hardness. Not like a real kiss at all.

As much as he felt it, *knew* it in his bones, Jeff wanted it to be real. He drew Audrey close for a second kiss.

She stepped away, a daub of pink on her pretty chin from the shaving foam mixed with his blood. He did that thing the delivery driver had done for him: he let her know. He pointed at her chin and said, you have a little something there. She seemed to ignore him. Instead, she waved, and walked down the short path, and walked down the street. Jeff watched her go, thinking about the kiss, thinking about the smile, thinking about the pink daub sat underneath it and why she had not wiped it from her face.

Jeff fought Nick on crazy golf for as long as he could but his son had come to know his own mind in the weeks since Hayley took him and went to live with Martin. He was decisive now, opinionated now. Hardened, like a rictus smile. Maybe it was the new male influence on the seven-year-old or maybe Nick had fast-tracked growing up in the frightening face of upheaval and uncertainty. He wanted the blue putter, to go first, to win against his father. He got all three.

After nine holes, they played a couple of classic arcade machines which Nick seemed underwhelmed by, then sat at a table in the tiki-themed games bar for a burger, a vanilla milkshake, a game of Jenga.

"Mum says we're moving to Oxford."

"When?"

"Didn't tell me. I heard her talking to Martin about it though. He has a new job there. Soon, I think."

"Soon, huh?"

"Is it far, Dad? Oxford."

"A couple of hours. Far enough. Do you want to go?"

"I don't know. I think so."

"Which is it?"

"Yes?"

"Is that a question?"

Nick shook his head. "I want to go. Is that okay?"

"It is what it is."

"Mum and Martin want to get married too."

Jeff sat his burger back on the plate, one bite out it. "It's a little soon, don't you think?"

"She says she loves him."

He knew it. The day of a thousand cuts. At least half of those would come from hearing those three words repeated in his mind throughout the next twenty-four hours. *She loves him.*

"What do *you* think? Is it a good idea, them getting married?"

Nick shrugged. "They seem really happy, Dad. Not like you."

"She told you that? I'm not happy?"

"No. No, she didn't have to."

They took it in turns then, pulling Jenga blocks from low in the stack, placing them on the top. The tower grew tall and unstable.

"Dad?"

"Yes, Nick?"

"Dad, why are you, like, sad all the time? Mum says she doesn't know."

"That's right, she doesn't. No one does."

"Will you tell me?"

Jeff shook his head for so long it was hard to stop.

"I can't do that," he said.

"Why?"

"I can't talk about it."

Nick ate some of his burger, chewing each mouthful slowly, painstakingly. Jeff saw him eyeing the shelves in the bar stacked with old board games.

"Do you want to play something else? I don't like this game." Jenga was about taking turns to move blocks around until it all came crashing down. The loser the one who made that happen.

Nick shook his head. "Do you know why they call them board games? Because they make you bored. I like Fortnite. I play it with friends. Do you have friends, Dad?"

Jeff shook his head as under the table he gripped the folding knife in his pocket. "I lost touch with all mine when I was a little older than you are now. There's a saying, about how you never have friends like the ones you had at twelve. It's true. It's from a film, 'Stand By Me'."

"I've never seen that," Nick said.

"Of course you haven't," Jeff replied, a little sharper than he intended. "It's probably not on YouTube."

"Everything's on YouTube, Dad. What time is Mum picking me up?"

"Why? Do you want to go? Come on, let's go."

Again, sharper than Jeff intended. Cold-tempered steel.

He got up, paid for the uneaten food, headed for the exit, knowing Nick was tight on his heels. Walking back, after school and friends and what Nick had been playing on his Xbox, there wasn't a lot left for them to talk about. It felt like their Venn diagram was pulling apart, or like this was the end of an eclipse when the Sun and the Moon returned to their respective orbits and the illusion of closeness was sadly revealed as just that. And while pre-seperation Nick would have volunteered pointless conversation, chatter *ad nauseum* Jeff had called it once upon a time in another story, it felt different now, like he was saving it for someone else. Martin, no doubt. Yep, he thought. The day of a thousand cuts.

"Anything else your mum has said about me?" he asked.

Nick looked up, searching the fading blue sky overhead as he bit his lower lip.

"It's okay to tell me. I'm sure it's nothing I haven't heard before anyway. Hit me."

"*Hit* you?"

"It means tell me."

"Oh. Well, she says you never go out. That you're a hermit."

Hayley could never understand how Jeff had not only liked lockdown, but welcomed it. We can't go out, she'd complain. To which he'd reply, But nothing can get in. Maybe that was the beginning of their end, he thought. The crucible of lockdown.

But long ago Jeff understood how, with that feeling of being trapped and time on their hands, everyone drew the same conclusion. Whether it was his mother running out on him and his father one week before his twelfth birthday, or Hayley looking for answers in another man, or himself, age twelve with the arrival of the black dog panting at his door – the same five simple words were drawn from the lexicon of unhappiness: *I don't want to be here.*

"I think you'll like it in Oxford," he said. "I think you'll make lots of friends and you'll have a good life up there. You should go. You *will* go. And you will be exceptional. Here, take this…"

Before he thought better of it, Jeff drew Nick off the pavement, into the doorway of a shuttered shop. He held out his hand. On his palm, the stockman he had been carrying in his pocket all day.

Nick's eyes widened and his face lit up.

"Wow! Is that for me? Dad, it's *so* awesome."

For a moment, it felt like old times. The circles of their Venn diagram overlapping. The eclipse not only happening but something beautiful and breathtaking and wild. But in those few short-lived moments of total darkness, Jeff could not see. And then the moment passed and he did. He saw his son's hand reaching out for what lay on his. Was this how it started? He thought. Was this his gateway drug into the world of knives?

"On second thoughts," he said, "maybe this isn't a good idea. You don't want this. Sorry."

"I *do*. I do want it."

"No, you don't. It was a stupid mistake." Jeff closed his fingers around the knife and slid it back inside his pocket. "Look, I can buy you a toy or something. Or a game. How about a game for your Xbox?"

Nick looked tearful and angry. "I don't want a game. I don't want a fucking game. Or to move to Oxford. Or to be living with Mum and Martin. I want *you*. I want the knife. Can I have it? Please, Dad. I'll be super careful with it, I promise."

Jeff pulled his mobile phone from another pocket, opened Contacts, found Hayley, called.

She answered quickly. Nick was with him and seeing Jeff calling she probably thought, something's happened. Mother's instinct. She wasn't wrong.

"You need to come collect him," he said.

"Why? What have you done?"

"He's fine, he's not hurt. He's just upset…about everything that's happened. Can you collect him?"

"Of course, but can't you calm him down? You're his father."

"I know what I am. He'll be fine by the time you come pick him up. I just can't deal with this now."

"You can't deal with your own son, Jeff? What the fuck?"

"This was your idea," he said. "Maybe you could have found another way of telling me you were moving away and getting remarried, Hayley. Like, you could have called or sent me a fucking email."

"I didn't know how else," she said. "You get so mad sometimes."

Jeff closed his eyes and felt the tears pushing at the backs of his eyelids. "It's not you, Hayley. It was never you..."

"It's too dangerous here," she said. "The knife crime is out of control. I just think he'd be safer if I took him out of London. It really was as straightforward as that."

"Hayley?"

"What?"

"I agree with you."

"You do?"

"I'd buy every knife if I could. If it meant it would keep him safe. But I can't and it won't." I've tried, he thought. "You're doing the right thing."

"You'll still see him though."

He looked at Nick standing beside him in the shop alcove, knuckling tears from his eyes and sniffing in angry disappointment. In ten or fifteen minutes, when Hayley drove away with him in the back seat and then proceeded to extract the story of how his father almost gave him a knife as a present, she would do the wise thing and retract any such invitation.

"Hayley?"

"Yes?"

"I knew it this morning."

"Knew what? What are you talking about?"

"That it was over," Jeff said. "Take our boy. Do what is best for him. God knows, you know better than me what that is."

Jeff gave Hayley the address. While Jeff and Nick stood side by side in the shop doorway, waiting, they watched the sun slip down the late afternoon sky as somewhere on the other side, out of sight of them, the moon began its steady rise.

I don't want to be here, they both thought on this, the day of a thousand cuts.

At seven o'clock, Jeff got ready for Audrey's arrival. Nick's mother had collected him hours ago and Jeff's phone had not vibrated in anger since so that could only mean the boy was holding out, so far. Maybe he would never tell. Secrets, like unread books, did not have to turn into stories; they could stay secrets forever. He tidied the house, putting knives in drawers and bagging the polyfibre from the dead settee in the living room. It had lain untouched for weeks, like snow refusing to melt. As there were more knives than there was drawer-space in the house, he carried armfuls of them up to Nick's empty room and laid them out in rows, covering the entire floor twice. One upon another. An orgy of knives. Afterward, he closed the door and made a mental note to keep Audrey out of there. She got it, got him enough, his reasons, but he realised the sight of hundreds of knives unintentionally laid out like they were fucking wasn't a shining endorsement.

He took a shower. It did not feel right on his skin. It never did. He washed in the shower and the microbeads in the gel felt abrasive, sharp even, like micro*blades*. No amount of lather helped, so he rinsed, got dried, dressed.

At eight o'clock, he heard a knock on the front door.

Audrey looked almost the same as she had earlier but with a few notable differences. The long floral skirt and white-sleeved top. Same. But she'd changed her sandals to something with a heel. The shoes made her taller, bringing her lips level with his. Her smile seemed less peculiar too, less like a stroke victim and more natural, like she'd remembered how to work the muscles of her face. Jeff relaxed and drank some of the wine she brought with her.

They sat on stools and looked at each other across a corner of the kitchen island as they talked and drank the wine until it was gone, until the last of the daylight had left the sky. Jeff lit an old candle he'd found earlier in the back of one of the cupboards, and they laughed together when he realised it was scented, the potent citrusy smell clearly why it had found the back of the cupboard in the first place.

"It feels like I'm trapped inside a lemon," Audrey joked. "Come on, let's go upstairs."

She led the way, using the stairs to showcase the sway of her hips, while he could not take his eyes from the zip tattoo on the back of her neck.

"When did you get that?" he asked.

"The scar or the tattoo?"

"Both."

"The scar was when I was eight. Drunk driving accident. The drunk driver in question being my mother. The tattoo – I was twenty-one, I think."

Without the collar of her red polo shirt to get in the way, he could see the teeth continued farther down her back. He imagined they went all the way to the base of her spine, ending just above her Venus dimples. He felt a stab of shame at that, at somehow *wanting* the terrible accident to have befallen her as a child to have given her such a scar. But the wine, the conversation, the laughter about lemons, the zip tattoo, all of it brought them to his bed, to inevitable kisses, to hands on each other, to a naked, shuddering climax.

Afterward, he took another shower. The water felt right on his skin. His skin felt right on his bones. His bones did not feel as though they belonged to someone else but to him—

Not Jeff.

The water went ice-cold, and he jumped back, out of the stream.

Panic rose in his throat as he stood naked and looked through the glass for the reassurance of a knife and realised there wasn't one near at hand. They were all drawered or lying on the floor of Nick's old room. He wrung his hands as he kept looking, searching anyway. He thought he heard panting close to his ear, spun around, backed into the shower, jumped at the touch of the water, of anything, on his skin. He thought of the time he was twelve years old, he thought *around* the time he was twelve years old, because he wasn't ready and yet he knew it was happening here, now; he was going in. There were bullies at school, a whole rotten group of them, and they began to circle the weaker boys like sharks smelling blood, tasting the easy spill. He thought about what he'd seen those kinds of boys do to the weak, the quiet, the ones who kept their mouths shut. He remembered how he bought a knife from his friend at school, his good friend from school Martin. Not the same Martin that Hayley became good friends with and more. That was one of life's Strange coincidences. It was just a penknife but something he hoped would deter the sharks. He brought the knife home and hid it inside a pair of socks in his drawer. But Dad found it anyway. Dad didn't lose his temper because he was still so sad and so lost after Mum leaving he didn't have anything left *to* lose. He thought about waking up later that night, after Dad found the knife, of being woken up with the penknife held to his neck, to the hollow they call the jugular notch. He found that out later when he went back over every detail of what happened. Every detail. Penknife to the jugular notch, Dad leaned in and spoke in his ear. He was breathless, panting like a dog. *Never tell anyone about this, okay? You keep your fucking mouth shut. But first you'll keep it open.*

You thought about the next day, how Dad made you eggs on toast and then took you to play crazy golf. Another Strange coincidence. You thought about how Dad never did the bad thing again because he killed himself three months later. He left a note: *You can't take it back.* Everyone wondered what *it* was. Not everyone. Not Jeff. Not you. You knew what *it* meant.

First you'll keep it open.

Keep it open.

Open.

You also knew it was all your fault. You brought the knife home in the first place because the bullies were circling. Circling like sharks. You'd seen what they'd done to other boys, the ones they knew would keep their mouths shut, and you had to have something to protect yourself when they came for you, because you *knew*, after what Dad did to you, they were coming, because there was no way you were opening your mouth to anyone ever again. No way. Not Jeff. You would keep the knife and you would keep the secret, because – and here is the part that cuts the deepest – as much as you did not like *that*, Not Jeff, you did like your dad sometimes, even most of the time, because a monster will always change back into a man, he does not stay a monster forever, not every moment, and knives did not hurt you if you did not use them and kept them secret. Like books never read. Stories never told.

Jeff stumbled out of the shower. Collapsed on the bathroom floor, shower hissing at his back. He crawled into the bedroom, sobbing, struggling to breathe.

Choking.

Found the empty bottle of wine on the bedside table.

The empty glass.

The empty bed.

The empty house, full of knives.

The Hanged Man

Conrad Williams

For a moment, when Conor awoke in the darkness of the room, he did not know where he was. He was momentarily surprised to find the woman lying next to him was not his wife. And then sense returned, and he realised. He was in Cardigan. On the bay. Manchester and his wife – his estranged wife – were four hours' drive away. he didn't understand what had disturbed him. But then he heard it again. A low, grinding sound, at the same time a noise that sounded both weirdly wet and dry; inside his head and without. He thought that his wife was with him after all. She was an habitual teeth grinder, especially in her sleep, but, listening carefully, it seemed a much more pronounced, somewhat deepset sound.

He put out a hand and Anna was there, so much quieter than Rachel. So much more still. He hoped her nightly thrashing had not been solely down to him and the unhappiness that had grown during the deterioration of their marriage (she would readily claim it to be so). He was convinced, and he made sure Rachel knew about it, that the stress of maintaining her affair was the main contributing factor to any bedtime travails.

So as not to wake Anna, he slid out of bed and padded to the kitchen, where he poured water into a kettle and set about making tea. He had never been one for trying to get back to sleep once wakened. He'd rather get up and do something constructive than lie there trying to force sleep back into his bones. It seemed such a waste of time. Better to be up and about, ahead of the curve, and, though getting through the day would be a struggle, relish the knowledge that the following night would guarantee him oblivion.

The sound of grinding had followed him out of the bedroom. What was it? He took a look outside but there was no moon; the darkness was total. He stepped out on to the decking, relishing the crisp embrace of the sea air and the rhythmic song of the tide against the beach.

Yes.

Such a small word. Yet it had brought him here. Anna was a woman he knew through a mutual friend, someone she worked with at the finance offices in the centre of Manchester, overlooking Central Library in St Peter's Square. They met at a desultory end-of-Covid party where the mutual friend had introduced him to her as 'this poor bastard who is going through the same shit as you'.

It transpired that their stories were remarkably similar. Anna had happened upon a message on her husband, Ian's, iPad that had spurred her to investigate.

"It was just a message that said 'Read me' but it was from a woman I didn't know. I opened it and there was a picture of her – and Ian – a selfie of them kissing in some restaurant booth, and a caption: 'I want you'. He tried to pass it off as something that had happened before we met – I know, can you believe it? – but he was wearing a shirt I'd bought him for his birthday. The fucking arsehole."

She'd asked him hours later, half a bottle of good Rioja inside them, what was the worst thing he'd seen, once he'd found her phone with its incriminating moment and had determined to plough through the messages swapped between Rachel and Martin.

"Christmas Day," he said. "Maybe six weeks after it had started. She sent him a message which said: 'I love your hands, your mouth, your dick'."

"Wow," said Anna. "Merry Christmas."

Talking about it with her didn't necessarily make it easier to deal with, but it helped. There had initially been the sense that he was all alone in his discovery, that he was the only person on earth coping with this unpleasantness. The fact that she had experienced a similar shock made them instant allies, struggling at the foothills of divorce, dreading the summit. It didn't seem inevitable that they would end up together, but when it happened he wasn't too surprised. It wasn't awkward either, the way they unloaded about their marital failures to each other, sometimes while they were undressing each other. Always, he gave her positive responses.

Shall we have chicken for dinner?

He really wanted fish. *Yes.*

Do you like lemon sorbet? I love lemon sorbet.

He hated it. *Yes.*

Do you like… Do you want… What if I…?

Yes… God, yes.

It was a month on when she sat down with him and gave him a strange, assessing look. "I think," she said, "that I'm going to take you to my secret place. I think I'm ready to do that. Would you like to do that?"

Yes.

She asked him to keep the following weekend clear and she picked him up in her Volvo at eight in the morning.

"Where are we going?" he asked.

"I have a holiday home," she said. "Wales."

He was thinking of static caravans and climbing over each other in the night to use the bathroom. When she pulled up outside a large house within a stone's throw of the sea, he turned to her and said: "You're fucking kidding me."

Inside there was a sunken lounge and a snazzy kitchen and four bathrooms.

"This is yours?" he asked her. "What… *all* of it?"

It turned out that she and her husband had bought the house during a period of good fortune. And when he did the dirty on her, she pressed him to let her keep the place as part of their financial settlement.

"I have a connection to this place in a way he never did. For him this was a Grand Designs episode. He wanted to bring in architects to turn it into a Bond villain's lair. It was about him flexing his wallet and saying: *Look at the size of my penis.* Give him credit, though. He didn't fight me over it."

The moment they were through the door, Anna changed. It was as if the house – or the house and the beach and its surrounding collars of rocks – had flipped a switch in her. She pulled out the clips in her hair and shook it loose. She kicked off her shoes and set about opening doors and windows, sighing like a woman whose lungs had been spring cleaned. After pouring them glasses of wine, she led him on to the expanse of decking overlooking the bay. She'd taken some wine and then drew him into a kiss, let some wine trickle into his mouth. Her lips were hungry on him, her mouth wider than he'd remembered it. He'd felt panicky, as if this was a different woman to the one he'd left Manchester with. He'd opened his eyes impulsively, as if to check, and she was staring straight into him.

Now he was able to smile at the memory, although their subsequent visits – this was their third – revealed a different side to Anna. It was as if she became untethered, unleashed, once within sight of the ocean. Movement dragged his gaze away from the water, and thoughts of her. A red kite soared over the trees, the wedge of its tail flicking as it adjusted its trajectory. It reared in the sky; it had spotted something. He watched the bird for a while before it dropped out of sight into clumps of gorse, and he felt a pang for the poor creature beneath. Pop out for a spot of breakfast and you get a side order of death. He shivered and thought about returning to bed, but something stayed him.

He knew what it was, but until now he hadn't wanted to confront the notion. Anna scared him a little. It wasn't just the character tweaks that occurred once she was under foreign skies; it was the suspicion that he was with a completely different woman, as if, during a comfort break at the motorway services, she had given her car keys to an unhinged doppelgänger loitering in the toilets. Her appetites changed too. In Manchester, when he visited her at her house, her lovemaking was reticent, shy, tender. She followed his lead. She acquiesced. In the bay, she played rough. She pushed him into position. She pulled his hair to make him go down on her. She told him what she wanted, and how it was to be. He couldn't help but make comparisons with Rachel, the woman he'd shared a bed with for twenty years. Rachel hated her nipples being touched or kissed, Anna craved it; Rachel tended to come predominantly in the missionary position, Anna needed to be taken from behind; Rachel used her mouth on him as a way to get him ready for intercourse, Anna was often keen for oral sex to be the main event.

He shivered. Fog was rolling across the bay. The shoulder of rock to the north seemed to prevent it from travelling further; it sank back across the water and huddled there, as if sulking. Is everything okay? Are you happy? Is your marriage over? Do you want to be with this woman?

Yes.

He shivered again. Cold. It was late May but the weather was not yet behaving. The two previous visits had occurred early in the new year, and his birthday weekend at the end of March. He wondered if he'd ever see this place with sunshine painting the walls. He went back inside, finished his tea, and built a fire in the grate. He couldn't remember when he'd decided on a year of saying yes, but it must have been shortly after Rachel announced that their relationship was over. A year now. But for one reason or another they had been unable to move on. Covid. Work commitments. A volatile housing market. Divorce would make them both worse off financially. It was convenient, for the time being, to remain together. He was in limbo, torn between two ways of being. His life with Rachel – dead, loveless, stained by her cheating and endless regrets – and a future filled with desire and excitement, but somehow just beyond his reach. He piled kindling and balls of newspaper, aware that what he was doing now – creeping around behind Rachel's back (he didn't feel ready to tell anybody about this new woman in his life) – was much the way she had lived her life over the past eighteen months, and he felt disgusted by that.

The fuel ignited, Conor waited for the flames to catch before adding a log. Its warmth spread, and he felt himself becoming more sanguine. He moved to the sofa and lay down, his eyes never straying from the fire. He tried to ignore the grinding noise, or to find its authorship elsewhere: in the crackle of the wood, say, or the wind in the eaves of this enormous house. He should go back to bed. Anna was there, her curves, her mouth… but this was good. Nice and warm. Yes. Yes.

He blinked and the fireplace was cold, the log black, reduced. The light was different. Anna was sitting to his side, holding a glass of water. She was regarding him with an amused expression. She had large, amber-coloured eyes. They shocked him, sometimes, the size of them. As if they might tip out of her face if she leaned over too far.

"Avast me hearties," he said. "How goes it in Annaland?"

"I was cold. I was lonely. Why weren't you there?" she asked. And he was put in mind of solemn hymns sung at school assembly, under the watchful eye of Mr Whitby, standing at the piano, waiting for someone to step out of line. *And the creed and the colour and the name won't matter…*

"Couldn't sleep. The lure of the sea was too great. I told you you'd hooked up with a guy who was eighty per cent octopus. And anyway, you wouldn't have known you were by yourself until you woke up."

"Don't tell me what you don't know."

He glanced at her. There was flint in her voice, the first time he'd heard it. They had yet to have any kind of falling out. So far it had just been cheeky rejoinders. Banter, as the kids would call it. Perhaps the start of some kind of power play, a pushing of the boundaries to see at what point tempers were lost.

"Shall I make us breakfast?"

She shook her head. "I prefer a walk before I eat. Especially when I'm here. You want to come?"

He didn't, but she'd asked the question and he only had one answer. He watched her while they pulled on boots and coats. She seemed aloof, her manner crisp and efficient. She didn't drop him a wink or smile at him. The lack of sleep sat in him, woolly and vague. He had to keep stifling yawns. A walk would do him good, he persuaded himself. And she couldn't keep up this frostiness, not when they'd be taking the coastal path. She would thaw, he knew it.

It was raining when they left the house. There was a thick, grey seam where the sky met the sea, like a charcoal picture smeared by the artist's thumb. They walked down to the beach where they picked up the path angling up to the headland, where hawthorn and gorse took over. Halfway up, she stopped to look back at the house. Conor followed suit. Its edges were blurred by the misting of rain. The amber lights inside beckoned him back. He felt cold. A year of saying no, next, he thought. The fire and a chunky glass of something warming was what they should be doing now. Not wandering up some rain-hammered hill.

They walked for half an hour past fields of caravans and isolated train carriages transformed into novelty holiday cottages. The land rose with them, until each glance out to sea was met by a view of sheer cliffs, fifty, sixty feet high.

"They go tombstoning around here," Anna said. "It scares the living crap out of me."

"Tombstoning? This isn't Acapulco."

"Tell the kids that. I have conniptions whenever I see the locals hiking up here in their wetsuits. Half of them are pissed, or baked."

"How can it be deep enough?"

"It isn't. But there's a spot, beyond the rocks, where there's a drop-off. Pretty much the only spot in the bay south of twenty feet."

"Beyond the rocks."

"That's the thing," she said. "You can't just dive off the cliff. You have to take a running jump in order to clear them first. Otherwise… splat."

"Jesus."

"Sometimes the cliff is closed off because if it's slippery, like today, it's impossible. There's talk about building some sort of promontory to, you know, negate the danger. It'll take a dead kid before they commit to it."

"Or shut it down permanently. This is the twenty-first century. Health and Safety and all that."

"Have you done it?"

"Done what?"

"Tombstoning?"

"Have you been listening to anything I just said?"

He didn't know what it was. Maybe she was having second thoughts about him. Maybe, as he had seen something different in her, so she had noticed an aspect of him that didn't chime with what she'd originally perceived. Where initially their conversations had been intense and interesting, now their lines seemed to be getting crossed. She didn't quite get what he was saying; he didn't quite understand her point. He wondered if she was regretting introducing him to this secret place of hers. She poured wine. He cooked dinner. She played music and danced a little, and he wanted her. In her clingy T-shirt and black knickers she was the antithesis of Rachel, who preferred to relax in jogging bottoms and cardigans, whatever music she was listening to enclosed within her headphones. He hungered after this woman who was so natural and giving, despite the tendency towards withdrawal.

"On the beach," she said, dodging his grasping hands. "I want to fuck on the beach."

"It's freezing," he laughed.

"Will you fuck me on the beach?"

They stumbled down the road in untied boots, raincoats clasped over half-naked bodies. A few stars were momentarily visible behind the scud of deep cloud. Wind made snakes of Anna's hair. Soft squares of orange light in some of the other houses overlooking the bay reminded Conor of lozenges of paint in a watercolour set. There were no other people that he could see. According to Anna, sometimes there'd be a late dog walker, or, if the sea was calm, a nutter in rubber having a moonlit swim, but not tonight. He was surprised to find himself disappointed by that. There obviously lived in him an exhibitionist. The thought of being watched while he had his way with this vivacious woman increased his ardour.

"Here," she said. "Now." It was difficult to hear her over the crash of the surf and the grinding noise.

"Do you hear that?" he asked. "Is there any machinery around here? Mining?"

"What the fuck are you talking about?" She shrugged off her raincoat and reached for him. Her hands were cold on his skin. Her own flesh was tight and nubbed where the wind had kissed it. He was shivering so much he could barely stand straight.

"I'm sorry about earlier," he said. "Asking you if you'd jumped off a cliff. Of course you didn't. I just… It was something to say."

"Shut up. Come here."

She guided him into the wet centre of her. He gasped at the heat. He couldn't deal with the intensity of her eyes. They seemed to search beyond the focus of him, into the meat of his head, the back of his skull, beyond. She was looking for something, it felt like. Hunting. He felt as if he was being fed to her, like some diabolical machine in a butcher's back room. He felt as if she was grinding him. He cried out, but the sound was lost to the wind. She increased her pace, perhaps enthused by his voice, and he clung to her, staring out at the sea to avoid those scouring eyes, and the effect they might have on him. He didn't want to dwindle within her, disappoint her. He focused on the water, and the creaming of the waves on the sand, the shapes the spume created as the tide was urged against the rocks.

There was a swimmer out there after all.

Anna was moving too violently against him to allow him to speak. She was chasing a climax that was evident in the way she was biting her bottom lip, clawing at his buttocks as if to absorb every last millimetre of him. He was close too. He could taste ozone at the back of his throat. Sand hissed across his exposed flesh, adding a strange, not unpleasant layer to their lovemaking.

The swimmer was emerging, but something wasn't right. He wasn't wearing a swimsuit. He was hunched over, dragging his limbs. Perhaps he had cramp, or had been stung; didn't Anna tell him that the bay sometimes filled with jellyfish? Nothing about the way the swimmer moved seemed right. He looked angular, disjointed, like a bag of skin with the bones put back in the wrong order. The clouds broke, allowing moonlight through. And he saw, as his orgasm rose within him, that he wasn't far wrong. The swimmer's limbs were broken and bent, in places rammed through the taut skin in splintered white exclamations, but somehow he was shambling through the sand, and his crumbling bones were pouring out of him to meet it: like attracted by like. He wondered if the swimmer was the author of the grinding noise he had been hearing. But that was madness.

"Do you hear it?" he yelled into Anna's ear. Her teeth chewed at his neck as she lost control. "Do you hear?"

Conor called out, but the swimmer was too far immersed in his own pain, or his dispersal into the beach, to notice. And then Anna was crying out too, and he was too concerned to not lose his footing and fall while she bucked and writhed against him. When he was able to return his attention to the swimmer, he was gone.

Later, they were wrapped around each other in a steaming bath, glasses of wine beaded with condensation in their hands. Exhaustion meant they did not move much, nor speak. Anna's huge eyes were fixed on Conor's limp penis.

"Don't stare at me like that," he said. "I'll get stage fright."

He had not gone to examine the stretch of the beach where the swimmer had disappeared. The cold was too cruel. They had snatched up their coats and hurried back to the house. Despite the heat of the bath, he still felt the chill in his bones.

"Will we ever be properly warm again?" he asked. "Or are we doomed to carry ice in our veins for all eternity?"

"You drama twit," she said. "You've clearly led a sheltered life. Cosseted since you were a babe-in-arms, I bet."

"Nothing wrong with comfort," he said. "Nothing wrong with room temperature and four walls."

"You could be describing prison. You are describing prison, actually."

"Home. This home. Any home."

"Out there is life. Adventure. Experiences. Snow and ice and miles on the clock. That's what it's about. Not meat and two veg, Match of the Day and a king-sized bed."

"Oh, I don't know. What's wrong with a bit of both?"

"I always find people are too quick to give in to creature comforts if the option is there."

"Right-o, Ranulph Fiennes. I'll pay for the helicopter to bring your shattered remains down from K2, shall I?" He regretted the quip even as he said it. The image of the deformed swimmer made him wince, despite it so obviously being a figment. "Anyway, you're sitting in an enormous bath in a gorgeous house, with a glass of chablis and a hot man with a high sex drive. What more is there? Knob off up a hill if you like. Have an experience. I'm staying here."

She pressed her toes into his belly. "You're funny," she said. "What was that you were saying, earlier? You know, when I was trying to enchant you with my pussy."

"You *were* enchanting me with your pussy. I'm still enchanted now."

"You kept going on about something. Some noise. You mentioned mining?"

He shrugged, drank some wine. "Ever since we got here, I've heard this strange grinding noise. It makes me think of dentist drills. It feels as if it's… inside me. But also not."

"Maybe vertigo?"

"Really?"

Now it was her turn to shrug. "Inner ear? Some odd headache-related thing? Maybe it's just your ageing limbs dredging up the effort to give your girlfriend a good seeing to."

Her use of the word 'girlfriend' gave him a jolt. He'd been enjoying her company so much, he'd neglected to consider what was developing between them, and what he was leaving behind. "Is that what you are? My girlfriend?"

She seemed momentarily embarrassed, as if she'd overstepped the mark. But then she frowned and pouted at him. "What would you call me? Your bit on the side? Your shag?"

"Yes. I mean no!"

"What?"

He closed his eyes. He could feel things getting away from him. "Obviously no. I'm just… I decided on a year of saying yes to everything. After the shitty time I've had. It was just a reflex response."

"That's dangerous."

"Maybe. But yes brought me you."

"What am I to you?"

He felt suddenly exposed, vulnerable. He wished he was sitting up in the bath, or that there were some bubbles to conceal him. It felt odd to be interrogated like this while he was naked. He wished he hadn't challenged her.

He stuttered over some conciliatory phrasing. *You mean a lot to me. I look forward to seeing you. I feel there's a connection.* But it felt as if he was trotting out words that her intense gaze could see right through. That frostiness returned. She drained her glass and stepped out of the bath. "Take as long as you like," she said, wrapping a large towel around herself. "I'm think I'll have an early night. Don't wake me."

He was as quiet as he could be when he slid into bed alongside her. He reached out to touch her and she was wearing pyjamas. He didn't know what to read into that. It was exhausting. Perhaps he shouldn't have leapt into what looked like another relationship before his previous one was even cold in its grave. Everything in his life was uncertain. He was neither one thing nor the other. Married/single. Happy/sad. Secure/untethered. Maybe he should just stop trying to understand and live for the moment. That's what dogs did, and they were never crippled by existential angst. At least, they didn't seem to be. Maybe in quiet moments they pined for a bone they lost years before.

"You're not wearing pyjamas," she said. He jumped at her voice.

"You are," he said. "I thought you were asleep."

"I can't sleep. I don't like how we left things tonight. I'm sorry." She sat up. "And the whole pyjamas thing. That can be remedied." She slipped out of her clothes and lay back down. Her eyes glistened in the ambient light and he was reminded of beached jellyfish cooking in the midday sun. He turned his head to stare at the ceiling.

"I'm sorry too. I can't let things go and enjoy myself. I've got to pick at things like a scab."

"We'll work on that," she said. She pressed herself against him. He felt her breath, hot against his shoulder. "But right now, there's something else that needs working on."

For a moment, when Conor awoke in the darkness of the room, he did not know where he was. He was momentarily surprised to find the woman lying next to him was not his wife. And then sense returned, and he realised.

"Shit," he breathed. Bad dreams clung to him like rotting barnacles to a rusted ship's hull, but he could remember none of the details. A shift of light and dark. A switch between heat and cold. Something like that. And always, the grinding sound, the sound of someone pulverising peppercorns in a mortar.

He checked his watch: 7 a.m. Despite the residue of his nightmare, he felt refreshed and hungry. Careful not to disturb Anna, he padded out of the room and headed for the kitchen, where glorious sunshine was flooding through the windows. He made himself toast and coffee, and chopped banana into a bowl of yogurt. Then he took a tray with a coffee pot and a mug up to Anna.

In the gloom he could see she was awake. Her arms were raised above her head, her breasts free of the duvet. It was a pose he found intensely erotic, but he balked because it was a pose Rachel had often assumed too. Rachel's breasts were much larger than Anna's. And whereas Anna's nipples were inverted – becoming erect only when induced to do so by fingertips or teeth – Rachel's nipples were always 'on duty'. Christ, he thought. How long before the comparisons stop. It was tiring him out.

He placed the tray carefully at the foot of the bed and opened the curtains, shamefully grateful for the blinding hit of light that would cause her to squint. He couldn't take her scrutiny any more. "I brought you coffee," he said.

"So I see. I don't drink coffee until I've eaten breakfast. Hashtag observant."

"Sorry," he said. "It's okay. I'll have it. I usually have a bucket of coffee at home before I'm able to function."

"Define 'at home'."

His neck prickled. Was she goading him? Or was she trying to initiate a discussion about their future? That might well be a good thing, but he didn't like the needle in her voice.

"It's just a figure of speech," he said. "I don't mean anything by it."

"I'm home," she said. "Here. By myself, or with you when I decide it. You're home… when?"

"I feel at home with you," he said, desperately trying to not sound like someone reading from a script.

"But you're in somebody else's house."

"Yes."

"Do you call the house where you live 'home'?"

He rubbed his face. "I do. But only because I have nowhere else to go."

"You could move out."

"So could she. I did nothing wrong."

"Do you ever think she had an affair because she felt there was something lacking in you?"

"Lacking?"

"Well, whatever. You know. She wouldn't have had an affair if she was happy."

"Neither would Ian, I'm guessing."

Silence spun out between them. There was the distant breath of the shoreline. The incessant grind. Conor wondered if he'd suddenly become sensitive to the agonised sound of time passing.

"Look," he said, finally. "I'm not looking for a fight. We both had enough of that. Maybe we're both on edge because we find ourselves at the start of something. I don't want to wreck that. I'm guessing you don't, either."

She pressed her lips together in what he hoped was a smile. "You're right. We're the victims here. I don't mean to put you on the spot. Maybe I'm just jealous that you refer to where she is as 'home'."

"That's not what I mean. It's a turn of phrase. It's where I physically am. It's not where I spiritually am."

"I can't fuck your spirit," she said.

"You raise my spirits."

"Do I?"

He leaned over and kissed her, thickly, on the mouth. He liked that she didn't drop her arms from their position above her head. She arched her back and her breasts pressed against him.

He said: "My God… you're a very sexy woman."

"I think you need to mix up your life a little."

"Oh, it's mixed up enough, I think."

"Go tombstoning."

"What?"

"Show me you've got the will to turn your back on what's easy in your life. Show me some willing to jump into the fire."

"I don't consider you to be the fire."

"I am though," she said. "Compared to her, compared to what your life is at the moment… I am."

"Anna…"

"Will you go tombstoning?"

The weather seemed to have been affected by his mood. The sunshine had been but a momentary relief from the previous day's fog. Dark clouds were massing now, and the temperature had dropped.

He could have just said no. Even as he marched down to the beach, straining to hear if her footsteps were echoing his, he was regretting storming out of the bedroom, slamming the door shut. Tell her it was just a stupid game to get you out of your comfort zone. Tell her to fuck off and grow up. But no. He was going to do it. He was going to show her exactly where the fucking fire was in their so-called relationship.

Halfway up the coastal path he looked back towards the house and saw her, naked, in the bedroom window, hands on hips. Was she smiling? He faltered, aware that he could be overreacting – they had been triggering each other the whole weekend – but he was too far gone now to back down. In the moment he decided that, he saw a failure in her confident posture. She seemed to slump. Her face became punctured with shadow. She moved away from the window.

He would come back from this stupid venture sopping wet, shaking like dog. And then what? Hot baths and whisky and more reassurances? They kept moving the goalposts but nothing was enough. Call her bluff. Live the year of yes.

He thought he heard a door slam, but the wind might have brought that sound to him from anywhere. He was wondering whether to make the jump in his trainers or bare feet when he heard her voice calling him. She must just be on the first part of the coastal path, maybe four hundred metres behind him. He couldn't make out what she was trying to say, beyond his name. Was that an *I'm sorry*?

Too late for 'I'm sorry'. They'd been apologising all weekend and then fouling things up again almost immediately the wounds were kissed better. "Actions speak louder!" he yelled. For a moment, the stridency of his voice cut out that persistent background grinding.

He reached the exit from the path that would take him to the cliff edge from which he would make the leap. It wasn't as if he'd never done anything like this before. Just not recently. It wasn't the kind of thing you did in your early fifties. Summers in the 1980s, he'd cycle with his mates to Slutcher's Quarry near the Manchester Ship Canal and repeatedly throw himself off the sandstone piles into cold, deep water. Sometimes the police would chase them off, but the greatest danger – or so it was passed around – was impaling yourself on the prongs of the old diggers abandoned in the water.

"Don't, Conor!"

He could hear her clearly now.

"Conor, leave it! Come back!"

Ask me not to do it, he willed her. *Give me a reason to say yes.*

"This is madness, Conor!"

Part of him suspected she was deliberately holding back from giving him that out. He didn't turn to her. He didn't say a word. He surprised himself by immediately launching himself from the edge of the world. How could he not when she was watching him? No dilly-dallying, his mum had often said to him when chasing him into bed on a school night. No dilly-dallying.

He hit the water two seconds later. The shock of the cold was immediately negated by a pain that flashed through him in an instant, to be replaced by complete numbness. Light had torn through his head. He tried to orient himself and strike for shore, but he couldn't move. He rolled in the water like a shark with its fins removed. The grinding was in him; he felt it in his neck when the waves shifted him, his flopping head now held in place by nothing more than calcium dust. He couldn't feel his arms or legs any more. He couldn't feel the cold. When he tried to cry out, saltwater filled his mouth. He could see her at the top of the cliff, before the tide turned him again and his eyes saw nothing but the black deep. Life/death; air/water. He waited. For once, an outcome was imminent.

Gary Budden
www.newlexicons.com

Dan Coxon
www.dancoxon.com

Malcolm Devlin
www.malcolmdevlin.com

Steven J Dines
www.stevenjdines.wordpress.com

Carly Holmes
www.carlyholmes.co.uk

Ida Keogh
www.twitter.com/silkyida

Alison Moore
www.alison-moore.com

Lynda E Rucker
www.lyndaerucker.wordpress.com

Jonathan Sims
www.jonathan-sims.com

Anna Taborska
www.annataborska.wixsite.com

Conrad Williams
www.conradwilliams.co.uk

www.blackshuckbooks.co.uk

Also available:

GREAT BRITISH HORROR 1:
GREEN AND PLEASANT LAND

FEATURING STORIES BY

JASPER BARK
A.K. BENEDICT
RAY CLULEY
JAMES EVERINGTON
RICH HAWKINS
V.H. LESLIE
LAURA MAURO
ADAM MILLARD
DAVID MOODY
SIMON KURT UNSWORTH
BARBIE WILDE

GREAT BRITISH HORROR 2:
DARK SATANIC MILLS

FEATURING STORIES BY

CHARLOTTE BOND
PAUL FINCH
ANDREW FREUDENBERG
GARY FRY
CATE GARDNER
CAROLE JOHNSTONE
PENNY JONES
GARY MCMAHON
MARIE O'REGAN
JOHN LLEWELLYN PROBERT
ANGELA SLATTER

Also available:

GREAT BRITISH HORROR 3:
FOR THOSE IN PERIL

FEATURING STORIES BY

STEPHEN BACON
SIMON BESTWICK
GEORGINA BRUCE
KAYLEIGH MARIE EDWARDS
JOHNNY MAINS
PAUL MELOY
THANA NIVEAU
ROSALIE PARKER
KIT POWER
GUY N. SMITH
DAMIEN ANGELICA WALTERS

GREAT BRITISH HORROR 4:
DARK AND STORMY NIGHTS

FEATURING STORIES BY

G.V. ANDERSON
SIMON AVERY
M.R. CAREY
PAUL M. FEENEY
KATH DEAKIN & TIM LEBBON
ALISON LITTLEWOOD
MAURA MCHUGH
PRIYA SHARMA
PHIL SLOMAN
CATRIONA WARD
REN WAROM

Also available:

GREAT BRITISH HORROR 5:
MIDSUMMER EVE

FEATURING STORIES BY

C.C. ADAMS
JENN ASHWORTH
SIMON CLARK
STEWART HOTSTON
RACHEL KNIGHTLEY
STEPHEN LAWS
LISA MORTON
LINDA NAGLE
ROBERT SHEARMAN
KELLY WHITE
ALIYA WHITELEY

GREAT BRITISH HORROR 6:
ARS GRATIA SANGUIS

FEATURING STORIES BY

STEVE DUFFY
BRIAN EVENSON
HELEN GRANT
MURIEL GRAY
SEAN HOGAN
ANDREW HOOK
SARAH LOTZ
LUCIE MCKNIGHT HARDY
TEIKA MARIJA SMITS
LISA TUTTLE
STEPHEN VOLK

Lightning Source UK Ltd.
Milton Keynes UK
UKHW041825030922
408285UK00002B/148

9 781913 038786